ALLŌS THE BLUE

MADISON STEVENS

SilverWood

Published in 2021 by SilverWood Books

SilverWood Books Ltd
14 Small Street, Bristol, BS1 1DE, United Kingdom
www.silverwoodbooks.co.uk

ISBN 978-1-80042-081-6 (paperback)
ISBN 978-1-80042-082-3 (ebook)

British Library Cataloguing in Publication Data
A CIP catalogue record for this book is
available from the British Library

Page design and typesetting by SilverWood Books

Prologue

A haunting drone of sirens rang throughout the still night of Heaven. A great conflagration enveloped the land as far as the eye could see, lighting up the landscape in a brilliant yellow. A thick layer of smoke suffocated the air, wrapping around the gleaming skyscrapers that adorned Heaven's skyline. The violent rumble of the flames was deafening to those unfortunate enough to be near them.

The local authorities, known as the Omegas, an elite team of ten archangels, speculated that this was a coordinated attack on Heaven. The question still remained: who had attacked Heaven?

One theory was that a bitter angel had found the ancient tomes of Lucifer's words deep within the archives and had become a devout disciple of his teachings. From that point, they had rallied many angels to their cause and led an invasion of Heaven, thus sparking the Second Demon War.

The Omegas were not expecting an attack, especially of that magnitude. This plan was well thought out. The rogue angel, as the Omegas called them, had attacked Heaven at every point, wiping out medical centers, supply depots, command centers, parts of the archives, and thousands of civilians, staining the streets red with their innocent blood.

Heaven had only seen an attack of this scale six thousand years earlier, during the Luciferian wars. The Luciferian wars were a bitter time for Heaven. That was a time in which angels betrayed their brothers and sisters, leaving raw memories that plagued the surviving angels to this very day.

Chapter 1

Witnessing this attack from atop one of the many skyscrapers adorning the skyline, anger surged within me. I closed my eyes, and upon opening them I felt a great surge of energy flowing through my eyes and my being. I inhaled deeply and spread my four wings. I stepped off the place I was perched and gently fell through the night sky. I had always loved flying ever since I was little. I loved the thrill of having such command of the skies. I landed in the streets that were blazing with fire and smoke. I could hardly hear anything, or see for that matter. That didn't stop me from helping as many as I could into the shelters scattered through the streets, all the while battling raging flames, smoke, and swarming demons.

I held out my right hand, palm open, and with a flash of light a magnificent glaive was in my grip. My glaive, from the base of the handle to the tip of the blade, was as tall as I was. I always admired how beautifully minimalistic my weapon was. It perfectly transitioned from the handle to its broad, tapered blade. I remember when my teacher Gabriel the Gold was so surprised when I chose the glaive. I knew that he wanted me to choose the mighty hammer as my weapon. To be honest, the hammer is too brutal for me. I'd rather cut down my opponents than smash them to bits. I always loved the spear and the sword, so I looked for a weapon that combined both elements.

At that moment a demon jumped from out of the fires with their weapon drawn. They charged at me with lightning speed, and I could sense such rage and hatred behind their attack. With a bloodcurdling scream, they plunged their weapon into my chest, causing me to bleed onto the streets. Upon impact I felt that I had a weight on my heart, and I could slowly feel my heart starting to wither away. Which is fine in some aspects because all angels and demons have a closed circulatory system of seven hearts, so I had some to spare.

The blade stung and it burned. This sting was familiar; it was the sting of an ethereal blade. An ethereal blade is the only weapon with the potential to kill any ethereal being. I didn't have time to use my glaive.

"In the name of God the Father, the Son and the Holy Spirit," I yelled, as I stared into the demon's pitch-black eyes and slammed my hand into its face, "go back to the deepest depths of Hell from whence you came!" With all my might I sent a pulse of fire completely through its face. The demon fell to the ground and burst into brilliant blue flames as it screamed out in pain while it burned away into oblivion, leaving only its weapon plunged into my chest. I pulled out the blade and I immediately started to feel relief and slowly started to return to normal. There was still an unbearable amount of pain pulsing through my chest.

"Damn, that hurt." I held out my palm and a pack of cigarettes appeared in my left hand. I brought one to my mouth and snapped my fingers and a small blue flame danced over my thumb. Just as I was about to inhale, two demons came barreling toward me, one to my left and the other to my right. The cigarette quickly burned away, and without hesitation, with my right hand, I plunged my glaive into the demon's heart. With a decisive flick of my left wrist, seven glaives sprung out from the ground and into the demon's hearts; the demon fell to the ground.

"Damned angels, you disgust me!"

I locked eyes with the demon and was taken aback. This demon must have recently turned. Its skin was still full of life.

"You're an angel. What are you doing? You're killing your own kind!" This demon-angel kicked me away and ripped the glaive from her chest.

It was particularly disturbing to me because I was able to recognize her. I knew this angel. Her name was Natalie. She and I would go drinking at the local bars around Heaven. We'd become friends over the years. She was so sweet and understanding, and had the prettiest eyes. I wonder what sent her over the edge?

"I am doing what is right! You keep us chained to the sky and force us to bend to meaningless rules!"

"Take that up with God. I am but a servant to his kingdom."

"Exactly. You blindly follow him," she exclaimed, as her nails started to grow.

Before I knew what had hit me, I felt my face sting. I touched my face and saw blood on my finger.

"You don't know what it is like, always questioning your loyalty, Allōs," she said, as she frantically started clawing at me.

I kept my distance, dodging her attacks in a way that resembled a graceful dance.

"I know that more than you would think, Natalie! You're forgetting my title as executioner. I have to kill demon after demon, and I sometimes question why. Like now, for instance! I don't want to hurt you, let alone kill you. Don't force me to."

"What about the angel that you killed just now?"

What? No, she's lying. Is she? I started to step away.

Natalie drew her weapon, which was a simple staff with

blades at each end. She then started mercilessly attacking. I tried my best to fend her off, but I was still thrown by what she had said. I mindlessly blocked her attacks as she chased me around the streets. *Did I really kill an innocent being? It's possible, but I don't see how that could have played out. Get a hold of yourself, Allōs!* I was so in my head hating myself for what I had done. I shook my head and focused. I took a deep breath and from my mouth a fury of fire barreled out of my throat. The flames pushed her back.

"Kill her," a quiet and distant voice said deep in the back of my head. I shook it off and focused on the fight in front of me. "I'm sorry, Natalie, but I will do what I must."

"You're going to kill me then?"

"If I have to, then yes."

"God will be displeased with you, Allōs," she said.

I noticed that the whites of her eyes were starting to turn black. It reminded me of a blotch of ink dropping on a white sheet of paper – the tiny black spot slowly creeping its way out, enveloping everything in darkness. Her eyes were completely black now. From that point I knew that she was too far gone in her hate and rage.

"Do it," the same voice whispered.

I can't, I won't.

"Do it, Allōs," it whispered again.

I had a bad feeling that if I didn't do what the voice said, I would end up dead. I took a deep breath and ended the fight. I swiped my hand upward and a large stone cross jumped from the ground. I pointed toward the cross, and Natalie went crashing backward into it. From the glaive I had drawn six more copies. The glaives floated out of the original and appeared in front of me. They circled around me gracefully and then they all pointed toward Natalie.

"Don't make me do this, Natalie."

"You said you will do what you must, so do it! Crucify me!" she screamed, with so much hate, she wasn't herself anymore. The kind, loving girl I knew was gone completely.

I nodded my head and the seven glaives quickly pierced all of her hearts.

"In the name of God the Father, the Son and the Holy Spirit, may you find peace, Natalie," I said, as I made the sign of the cross in the air in front of me. With that, a small blue dot appeared in the middle of her chest. It pooled out more and more until she was completely enveloped in blue. I snapped my fingers and she vanished, leaving her armor, her weapon, and a large scorch mark as her only surviving memory.

"Allōs!" Without thinking I sent a fireball through the tips of my two fingers in the direction of the voice.

"Ha, you missed me!"

I would have recognized that soft English accent anywhere. It belonged to Noah the Emerald.

"Oh shit, sorry, Noah!"

He approached me and immediately noticed that something was off. "You're trembling. What's wrong? It must be bad. I haven't seen you like this since you and Luke were fighting a few years back."

"Am I glad to see you!" I said, as I grabbed him by the arms and hugged him as hard as I could.

"Allōs, what's wrong? You're never like this in battle. Wait, where's Luke?"

"I don't know, but that's not why I'm upset."

"Then what's bothering you?"

I didn't know how to bring myself to say this, but I knew I had to. Would Noah hate me for this? I hoped not. But what

11

if he did? Would he report me? Would I get court-martialed? Or would something worse happen? I did what I had to, and she did turn, so there was a good reason behind her death. *Why am I freaking out over this? Get a hold of yourself!*

"Before I tell you, let's take care of these fires, shall we?" I turned around to face the fire and I started to breathe. With each continuous breath I raised my hands on the inhale and lowered then on the exhale. A few moments into my breathing the conflagration started to rise and fall with my breath. I could feel the fires burning with pain. I inhaled deeply and then suddenly cast my hands down, which snuffed out the raging flames all around us.

"I forget how powerful you are at times, Allōs," Noah commented.

"Nah, fire and I just get along." I swirled one of my hands and a pack of cigarettes appeared. I put one in my mouth and snapped my fingers and blew out a small puff of smoke. "Noah, do you remember Natalie?"

"Your friend?"

I took a drag and exhaled. I nodded.

"What about her?"

"She's dead. I had to kill her."

"What do you mean?"

"She turned, Noah. Her eyes went black – I saw it! I don't know what sent her over the edge, but it must have been huge for her to turn like that. Not to mention the whisper that I heard telling me to kill her. I didn't want to, honest to God I didn't, but I knew I had—"

"Al, you're spiraling. Just breathe. You did the right thing, Al. Something else is bothering you."

"I can't shake something she said out of my head. She said, 'What about the angel that you killed just now?'"

12

"Allōs, she said that to get to you." Noah ran his finger through the scorch mark on the street.

"Do you really think so?"

"I know so. Why are you doubting yourself?"

"It happened so quickly, I didn't have time to see what was going on – I just reacted. I don't want to talk about it anymore. I need to talk to the Omegas." I turned away.

"About? Mate, you alright? I'm not going to let you go anywhere until I know you're okay," Noah said, as he turned me around by the shoulder.

"It's nothing that I can't bounce back from." I took another drag while embers started to form around me and gently swirled about. As they danced around they got brighter and hotter until they burst into blinding blue flames that engulfed me in a vortex of fire. I held up my two fingers and cast a lightning bolt into the sky. It exploded into a colorful array, notifying the Omegas to assemble. Noah spread his wings. I'd forgotten how beautiful Noah's wings are, and Noah in general for that matter. He was sculpted like a statue that even Michelangelo would be jealous of. He was a tall fellow with short blonde hair and piercing blue eyes. Then you have me: I suppose I'm beautiful in my own right. I always felt that I stood out as an angel. All of the Omegas are gorgeous, with porcelain skin and pure white wings, unlike me. I am olive-skinned and have wings black as night. For as long as I can remember, I have always hated my wings. I thought they were the wings of a demon. Mother always told me that the reason behind my wing color is that black wings signify hardship in a past life. Which makes sense since I was stillborn on Earth. Then I was given a second chance at life. So, I grew to love my wings.

I spread my wings and Noah and I pushed off, rocketing toward a two-towered skyscraper to get an overview of the destruction. This building was a beautifully neo-futuristic sky-scraper which blended into the hillside because of its mirrored panels. This tower stood ten stories high. The right tower is used for storage of the Omegas' records, dating back to the Luciferian wars. The left pillar contained the living quarters for the Omegas in order of rank.

We flew into a massive open window and arrived at Gabriel's chamber door. Noah and I were greeted by lifelike images of Gabriel posing triumphantly over a gleaming landscape on two large golden doors. I let my cigarette burn away before we entered Gabriel's chambers.

"Ugh, Gabriel, you just love self-portraits, don't you?"

"He really does, doesn't he?" Noah said. "But they are amazing nonetheless."

I smiled as we pushed past. The room reeked of cigar smoke. To some it would be off-putting, but I had gotten used to the smell and had grown rather fond of the scent. Gabriel's chambers were very spacious and covered tastefully in gold; portraits of him hung proudly on the walls. Three massive windows stood in front of me, and two to the left and right of his golden doors, peering over Heaven perfectly. In front of the northern window rested a writing desk that had papers, maps, and liquor strewn about the surface, while large wingback chairs were at opposite ends of the desk.

"Allōs, Noah, always good to see you two," Gabriel said with a warm voice. He seemed oddly relaxed and nonchalant given what was happening outside. "Oh, Allōs, I want to commend you on snuffing out the fires all through the town square. Most impressive."

"Oh, thank you," I said, as I bowed slightly.

"No need to bow, Allōs, though I appreciate the sentiment. By the way, why did you call a meeting?"

"Something happened that I'm not yet comfortable talking about. Noah can fill you in on the details. I need to see familiar faces that haven't turned. I need that peace of mind, Gabe."

Gabriel sighed and pulled a cigar from his desk, cut it, and snapped his finger, and a small yellow flame danced above his thumb. He said, "In turbulent times like these, Allōs, you will see and do things that will question everything and rattle you to the bone. Especially for those as young as you and Noah. But, Al, take solace in this – whatever you had to do, it was the right choice." Gabriel rose from his chair and looked at me with his blue eyes and went to the window to the left of the room. After taking a drag, he blew out a continuous puff. From out of that smoke a large storm cloud formed and released torrential rain that quenched the fires throughout Heaven. Gabriel brushed his flowing golden locks out of his eyes. "You boys look like you need a drink," he said, and he poured one for Noah and me. "Allōs, aside from having a therapy session, why did you call us?"

"Oh, because I want to get to the bottom of what started these attacks. Who did it, why, that kind of stuff."

"Nice save."

Out of the corner of my eye I noticed multiple figures fly through the window. I started to make out the forms of the Omegas, which consists of Michael the Scarlet, Raphael the Amethyst, Jophiel the Auburn, Azrael the Royal, Chamuel the Pewter, Ariel the Onyx, and Luke the White.

"Allōs, you called?" Michael asked. "Did you put out the fires as well?"

"Only in the town square. The rest was Gabriel."

"Do you realize how big the town square is? That's not a simple feat. That's most impressive. Gabriel taught you well."

Another voice jumped out at me. "I didn't come to this meeting to shower Allōs in compliments! Why are we here!?" Chamuel barked, as he slammed the bottom of his spear on the floor, causing a soft rumble.

"You know why we're here. We all know why we're here. Stop antagonizing Allōs, Chamuel," Jophiel replied.

Chamuel bit his tongue and grunted.

"Allōs, what happened to your face? Did something claw at you?" Jophiel asked.

I fell silent. I touched my face and it was still sore. "Yeah, I don't want to talk about it. It's too upsetting." I quietly took a sip of the drink Gabriel had offered. I set the drink down and pulled a cigarette from the air and lit it. I said, "I called you all here for a number of reasons, but mostly I want to get to the bottom of this attack, and bring this person down. Not to mention that we need to evaluate the amount of damage that has been done, make a head count and future contingency plans for further attacks and so on and so forth."

"Future attacks?" Ariel the Onyx asked. I could tell by Ariel's eyes that I was about to confirm her fears.

"I believe so. No one launches an attack of that magnitude without coming back. Chamuel, I think that you should be satisfied with why I called this meeting."

Chamuel stuck his tongue out at me. "Perhaps I underestimated you, young one. You actually thought something through this time."

"Have some faith in me. I am here for a reason. Gabriel, do you have any information that we can work with?"

"I don't have any specifics, but this angel killed enough people and destroyed enough property to spark a war. I haven't seen an attack like this since the Luciferian wars. Peter should be here momentarily with specifics." Gabriel offered the rest of the group a drink and we toasted to the Omegas.

Then there came a knock on the door. Gabriel waved Peter in. He came holding a small scroll with a golden seal binding it shut. Gabriel nodded to Peter and scanned the scroll.

"Noah, you haven't said a word. Everything alright?" I asked.

"Yeah, of course. I'm just worried about you, Al."

Noah is the quiet one of the group who likes to keep to himself. He normally spends his time in the archives burying his head in books all day instead of socializing.

"How many people died?" Ariel asked.

Gabriel glanced through the scroll. "Six thousand deaths, and eight thousand injured."

"What should we do?" Luke asked.

"I'm with Allōs on this one. We need to start planning for further attacks," Raphael interjected.

We all nodded.

Raphael is an interesting angel. He is the most militaristic of all of us, but you would never guess it based on his personality. Raphael is a calmer and more approachable angel than Chamuel, but at times he likes to think with his fists.

"There is one glaring issue that we still have to figure out. We have no idea what this angel looks like," Jophiel said softly.

"How the hell are we going to find that out?" Azrael said.

"I have an idea. We could all go to the Omni Realm at the exact moment and go from there," I suggested.

"That's incredibly well thought out, Allōs. Why didn't I think of that?" Azrael said.

"Yeah, that's an idea," Chamuel agreed, as did the others.

"I'll need two people to stand guard."

"I'll volunteer, Gabriel." Raphael stepped out of the circle.

17

"As will I," Ariel proclaimed.

Luke raised his hand hesitantly.

"Yes, Luke?" I nodded to him.

"I feel like I should know this by now, but what is the Omni Realm?"

"Oh, that's right! You've never been. It's time travel, but you can only interact with your surroundings. Consequence-free, of course."

"Huh, convenient."

"Indeed. Now, angels, gather around. If any of you wish to leave, do so now." The entire room was silent as eyes darted around the room from angel to angel. "Great, let's get started."

One by one each angel closed their eyes. Upon opening them, their eyes were glowing an ethereal white – all of the angels except for Luke.

"Luke, you have nothing to worry about. You'll do fine."

"Allōs, I'm just nervous, because I don't know what to do."

"That's what he said." I chuckled, with a cheeky wink.

"Fuck sake, Allōs." Luke slapped my chest and rolled his eyes as I smiled.

"You'll be fine. I promise it's easier than one would think. You're not part of the Omegas for nothing," I said, looking into Luke's emerald-green eyes.

"You know what the timeline looks like, right?"

He nodded. "Yeah, it's that thin golden line, right? Al, I've tried time and time again, but I just can't seem to get to the void. My eyes usually just roll to the back of my head and nothing happens from that point."

"Luke, just remember what I taught you and you'll do fine. Think of nothing but the present moment and imagine the golden thread and everything will fall into place," Ariel said.

"You'll be transported to a void and you'll see us. I'll explain the rest when you get there, okay?" Luke nodded as I put my hand on his shoulder and couldn't help but ruffle his hair. "You're just adorable, you know?"

"Nah, you." Luke smiled as he brushed a misplaced hair out of my face.

"Are you two done flirting? Get going," Raphael said.

Luke took a deep breath as he nervously looked around the room while Raphael and Ariel gave an encouraging smile.

"Here we go," I heard him whisper to himself as he closed his eyes, trying to tighten his focus. When he opened them again, they were rolled into the back of his head. The three of us held our breath while Luke twitched until he straightened and his eyes lit up like a lighthouse.

"There we go, Luke." I put my cigarette in the closest ashtray and closed my eyes. Upon opening them, I was in the void. "It's about time you got here. I hope you two had fun."

"It takes me much longer than five minutes, Noah."

"I'm proud that you can actually take your time, Al." Gabriel chuckled.

"I didn't realize my sex life fascinated you so much."

"Hey, I'm going through a dry spell. What can I say?"

"Noah, I thought you were with Taylor. What happened to him?"

"Yeah, we broke up a few months ago."

"Ah, that makes sense. You've been more irritable recently. Moving on, let yourself be known by name if everyone's present."

"Gabriel."

"Michael."

"Azrael."

"Chamuel."

"Jophiel."

"Noah."

"Luke."

"Good. Now that we are all here and accounted for, we can start to figure this out."

"But where do we start, Al? We have no idea where this angel attacked."

"I do, Luke. According to the scroll I received earlier, the rogue angel and their accomplices attacked multiple places at the same time," Gabriel said.

"What were the places that were attacked?" Azrael asked.

"Bits and pieces of the archives, medical centers, supply depots and command centers, and thousands of civilians. So nothing that we didn't already know," Gabriel replied, as he brushed his golden locks out of his eyes.

I said, "Take us to them." A spike rose in the timeline and within a blink of an eye we were in a large room with high ceilings.

"Where the hell are we?" Raphael asked.

"Let's find out." I swept my arm upward and every torch in the room lit itself. This room was a sight to behold. The entrance was lined with statues of the apostles standing sentinel, mirroring each other. Past the apostles, in the center of the room, a gilded clock hung in midair as it softly ticked away the time.

I had forgotten how beautiful this building was. It was a perfect blend of Gothic architecture with a futuristic flair. I couldn't help but be lost in the grandeur of the building. Millions of books lined the seemingly endless shelves that crawled up the walls and encompassed the entire room, which was bathed in blue lighting from the torches.

"We're in the archives," Noah said.

We were all taken aback by the scale of the building. I couldn't help but feel so tiny. I remembered this feeling from when I was a kid wandering around this massive collection of knowledge.

"Just how big *is* this place?" Luke exclaimed, awed by the magnitude.

"Four hundred and sixteen feet by one hundred and fifty-seven feet. The columns stand at fifty feet on each level, then it's another twenty feet for the arches. Got all that down, Luke?" Noah asked.

"Uhhh, I think so, Noah," Luke muttered.

I looked around to get the lay of the land, and glanced at the clock. Its face showed 10:28am and then swiftly rewound itself to 8:46am before my transfixed expression.

I pointed to the clock and said, "Am I seeing things or did that clock just change?"

"Are you feeling alright, Allōs? I know you're shaken up and all, but you okay?" Gabriel asked, looking concernedly at me with a puzzled look on his face. "I didn't notice anything."

"I swear I saw the clock change, Gabriel."

"It's impolite to swear in front of company, Allōs."

"I fucking saw it, I know I did."

"So what? Do you really think that would warrant telling anyone? Come now, don't be crazy, Al," Chamuel said.

"Now, now, Chamuel, we all know he's crazy, but that's beside the point right now," Jophiel intervened.

The room shifted focus back a couple of minutes to when the clock had changed hours. The angels looked on in interest while Luke glanced around, looking at the others' reactions.

"Ta-da! Asshole." Gabriel smiled wryly. "Alright, fan out and enshroud yourselves in the shadows."

The angels nodded and enabled their armor. Their armor enveloped their skin in thick liquid and solidified around them.

Each angel summoned their corresponding weapon. We dispersed throughout the top and bottom levels, among the books and columns. I summoned my glaive and hid deep within the shadows. I waved my hand and all of the torches went out, leaving us in darkness. The room became enveloped in silence. After a while, the silence became unbearable. The only sound that I could glom onto was the ticking of the clock, and my own heartbeat. After what seemed like hours, the clock face became backlit and immediately struck 10:28am.

The time had come. The archive doors were flung open. A figure advanced through the room, its footsteps echoing off the high ceiling while the torches came alight in the figure's wake. I watched the figure get closer to my position and waited until it was level with me. I snuck about trying to get behind it, and when the moment was right, I grabbed its shoulder and turned it around to face me. The moment I locked eyes with this figure everything went white.

I was thrown back into the doors of Gabriel's chambers. My head was spinning and everything hurt from hitting the doors. Raphael and Ariel picked me up off the floor and helped me to my feet.

"What happened?" Ariel asked.

"I have no idea," I said. "I think someone lost focus." I looked around and it appeared that everyone had felt a similar shock.

Gabriel, in his golden armor, gestured to Ariel and asked, "What is the current situation outside?"

"No new fires, sir. There are reports flooding in of demons swarming the northern half of Heaven, and we've sent troops to dispose of them immediately."

"Very good, Ariel." Gabriel sighed as he slumped down in one of his chairs and picked up the half-smoked cigar and reignited it with a quick snap of his fingers. After reaching for a bottle of liquor, he opened a drawer and put a glass on the desk and poured himself a drink. I picked up my drink and took a sip.

"This doesn't make any sense. How did we lose contact like that, and so violently? Speaking of which, are you okay, Allōs?"

"Yeah, I'm fine, Gabe. I probably have a concussion. Thank you for asking though."

"Ah, so nothing major."

"Was that supposed to happen?"

"No, it wasn't. Never in all my time have I ever experienced something like that before." Gabriel sighed and sipped his drink. "Even if someone lost focus, we shouldn't have come back to my chambers. We would have come back to the void. Those are the rules of the Omni Realm! That's how it works! This makes no sense," Gabriel ranted. He paused, taking a drag from his cigar. He handed me my cigarette from the ashtray and I relighted it and inhaled. Gabriel flicked his hand in a circular motion and nine wingback chairs appeared.

"All of you, be seated." We did as we were instructed and Gabriel continued to theorize. "Someone had to have disconnected all of us from the Omni Realm. That's the only explanation that I can think of, or that some third party joined without our knowing and disconnected us."

"What do you mean, Gabriel?"

"Well, Azrael, I've only heard stories, but the only example I can think of was during the Luciferian wars. However, it takes a skilled person to pull that off. The question is who. Ugh, all of you get some rest. We'll meet back here tomorrow morning."

We all nodded and dismissed ourselves. I hit the streets and was startled when Luke ran up and hugged me from behind.

"Some mission we had. What happened though?"

"I don't know, babe. It was weird. That shouldn't have happened."

"It was probably a fluke – nothing to worry about."

I grabbed Luke by the shoulders and looked deep into his eyes. "This wasn't a fluke. I guarantee someone disconnected us from the realm to hide something. I know it sounds crazy, but I believe it to be so."

"Allōs, everything should be fine. Let's get some rest."

Luke and I walked home, and when we got to the apartment, I slumped onto the couch and pulled Luke on top of me and held him in my arms. Luke rested his head on my chest while I played with his hair.

"I love you, babe."

"Love you more." He looked up and noticed faint marks on my face.

"What happened to you, Al? Your face is covered in scars."

"Oh that. A demon clawed at my face. Nothing to worry about."

Luke looked at me, knowing that I was telling him an absolute bullshit story. "Babe, what happened?"

I sighed and held on to Luke's hand.

"While I was putting out the fires in the town square, I was forced to kill Natalie."

"What happened to Natalie?"

"She turned. I saw her eyes go black. It was scary to watch a friend turn against you."

"Oh, shit. I'm so sorry that you went through that, babe." Luke knew I was hiding something else from him. "Al, you have more, I can tell."

"Natalie said something that bothered me."

"Which was?"

"Before we started fighting, she said, 'What about the angel that you killed just now?' And yes, before you say anything, I know I killed someone, but I don't know who or what it was."

"Babe, you saw her eyes go black, what more do you want?"

"You know that I'm not a killer. I would never kill a fellow angel."

"Did the other 'angel' attack you?"

"Yes, they rushed me to my left and right."

"Babe, you have nothing to worry about, in my opinion. I know you're beating yourself up over it, but trust me when I say, you did nothing wrong. Both of them had turned at that point. You did what you had to. No one said this was easy. Allōs, I know that you're not a killer. That thought never crossed my mind."

"Thanks, babe."

"You're still shaking, Allōs."

I pulled Luke into my arms and held him there. "Just hold me." Luke held me in his arms and I finally started to feel relief.

"You know it's okay to cry, right?"

"Shhh." I started running my hands up and down his body. Luke pulled the back of my neck and gently kissed me. I pulled him deeper into my chest as we lay on the couch for hours. I felt myself going to sleep.

When I opened my eyes, I was chained to a wall by my arms, legs, and neck. I pulled on the chains, trying to move, but I couldn't. I felt a rage build deep within me and the chains started to rattle and glow. The more the chains rattled the hotter the metal became. The metal dripped to the floor and the commotion attracted the attention of guards flocking toward me. They tried to subdue me, but nothing could stop me from escaping. I tried to fight my rage, but it was too powerful.

I summoned my glaive and cut down everything in my way. The bodies fell to the floor, bursting into flames. I kept cutting everything that came my way. The rage boiled in my heart and I felt my eyes being filled with energy, but it was different this time. I felt hatred in my eyes.

A hooded figure came up to me, and his presence and aura were something I've never felt before. His aura was dark and menacing, and it put me on edge. Simply looking at this figure spiked my anger. I swung my blade at him frantically and he caught my blade and broke my weapon.

I opened my mouth and a hellfire of blue came firing out of my throat. The figure stood there silently and absorbed the flames in the palm of his hand. He then pinned me to the wall by the throat and stripped me of my shirt. He opened his hand and a branding iron appeared. The iron began to glow red-hot. I was shuddering as the heat-soaked iron inched its way closer to me. I tried to push back, but I was frozen with fear. I couldn't move! I could feel the heat bouncing off my eyes and chest. Upon initial contact there was no pain – in fact, it was cold. Slowly, I felt a searing pain starting to pool in my chest. The pain became unbearable and I tried screaming, but nothing would come out. The figure disappeared just as quickly as it had come.

I was alone, surrounded by corpses and my thoughts. My thoughts were scattered about. I saw things that didn't make sense to me: I saw myself being trapped in my body, not being able to move for months. There were fiery images of ruined landscapes with someone dying in my arms. I saw another person lying in a pool of blood while covered in a shroud. I heard a haunting cackle reverberate in the room and then I gasped as I woke up.

"Oh, thank God, it wasn't real!" I was breathing heavily while locking Luke in my arms.

"Al, what's wrong?"

"Nothing, just a bad dream is all."

"What was it about?"

My chest was burning and it was agonizing. I gently pushed Luke off me. "Fuck, my chest hurts."

"What's wrong?"

I touched my chest and winced at the pain. I've felt burns in the past before, but none like this. I tried to talk, but I could only focus on the searing pain on the left of my chest.

"I don't know, babe. I guess I was burned." I removed my shirt and saw a risen mark that was burned onto my chest. I couldn't make it out though. I went to the bathroom and stood in shock. The mark of the omega encased in a circle stood proudly on my chest.

"What the fuck is that? This can't be good."

Chapter 2

I walked back into the living room and showed Luke what was on my chest. He was shocked and fascinated at what he saw.

"Hey, Luke, what is this?"

Luke got up from the couch and came in for a closer inspection. "I'm not sure. It's definitely a brand. How did you get it?"

"Remember that bad dream that I had?"

"You got it from there? I did find it odd that you fell asleep. That's out of character for you."

"Tell me about it. Nothing good ever happens when I sleep."

"Yeah, you and sleep don't seem to get along, but how did you get the brand?" Luke poked and prodded my chest and I hissed with pain. "This should help the pain." Luke placed his hand on my mark and it started to glow, and I immediately felt relief.

"I forget how magical your hands are at times. But to answer your question I got it during a dream. Some hooded figure branded me and I woke up."

Luke looked down and started biting his nail. I felt him start to panic. I hate it when Luke gets like this. It always put me on edge.

"You went to Sueniros Asparia."

That name sounded familiar, but I couldn't place where I had heard it. "What?"

"The dream realm. I didn't realize that things could travel from that world to this one. However, that realm is very tricky and can lead to very negative things, according to the archives." Luke noticed the look on my face, "Babe, hey, look at me. You're going to be fine, trust me."

"Then why are you concerned?"

Luke hesitated, trying to gather his thoughts. "Because I've read stories where demonic possession can occur in said realm. However, that's very rare, but it can happen. It's highly unlikely that you were possessed, but I can't take it off of the table either."

I stood there in shock at what Luke was saying. I didn't know what to say. I felt my hearts sink to my stomach. He buried me in his chest. I wrapped my arms around him and held him close. "I need to talk to Gabriel."

"I'll come with you."

I nodded and I got dressed, and Luke and I hit the streets. We spread out our wings and flew to the tower and landed in Gabriel's chambers. Upon arrival, I looked at his doors and hesitated to knock. I walked away and Luke pulled me back by the wrist.

"Allōs, I know you're scared, but you have to face this."

"I can't, babe. I'm not just scared. I'm terrified at the thought of this. Luke, I feel as if my world is about to crumble before me. Next thing I know is that someone is going to replace me as executioner and kill me as I did Natalie earlier today."

"Allōs! Get a hold of yourself! You know you're nowhere near that mark, understand? I know you're terrified, but you need to look at the facts of the matter. Are your eyes black?"

"No."

"Then why are you worrying?"

"Because I feel there's a chance I could turn."

29

"Allōs, let's deal with absolutes. As we are standing here the absolutes are this: You went to sleep, you were branded in your dreams, you woke up, and now you have a brand on your chest. That's it, so let's talk about the facts. Allōs, I have no clue what you're feeling right now, but I need you to remember the facts."

"Thank you, Luke."

"That's what I'm here for, Allōs."

I looked at the doors and back at Luke and knocked.

The doors opened and Gabriel turned from his desk.

"Luke, Allōs, always a pleasure to see you two! Take a seat wherever you would like. What can I do for you?"

"Am I bothering you?" I asked, as I sat down in one of the chairs that circled his desk.

"Not at all. You seem troubled. What's wrong? Oh, before we start, Noah filled me in on everything, and I'm deeply sorry that you had to go through that. You did the right thing though. Is that why you're here?"

"No. I have some other concerns about a dream I had, but we can discuss that later. What do you know about Sueniros Asparia?"

Gabriel paused and picked up his cigar. "It's the dream realm. It's a tricky place. Its main purpose is to communicate with other beings and bring things into reality from there. Why?"

"I was in a dream and a figure branded me with this…" I lifted my shirt.

Gabriel's eyebrow lifted in curiosity. He leaned in and ran his fingers over my brand. "Hmm, I haven't seen one like this before. Usually they look like tattoos, but I am jumping the gun. I can't say for sure – I need more information. What happened in this dream of yours, Al?"

I pulled down my shirt. "I was in an uncontrollable rage.

30

I killed everything in sight. After my murder spree, this hooded figure branded me."

Gabriel leaned back in his chair and puffed his cigar and twirled his hair nervously around his finger.

"Gabe, what is on my chest?" I asked sharply.

"I have an idea, but I'm curious to see if Luke and I are on the same page, and judging by your face, Luke, you know what it is."

"I think it's a seal. I could be wrong though but based on the information, it seems very likely that it would be one."

"I would agree."

"Is anyone going to fill me in on what's going on?"

"Demonic seals are the mark of a demon. It's essentially its coat of arms, Allōs. It's actually a very well-thought-out system if I'm being honest. But this isn't any seal I've seen. Whoever marked you made this seal specifically for you. It's incredible. However, this isn't good, Allōs. I was afraid this might happen at some point. I didn't expect for it to be so soon."

"You knew about this," I yelled, as my eyes burned, before the feeling quickly faded. I realized that the same feeling that I had in the dream was slowly creeping into my system.

Gabriel placed his hand on my shoulder, and I started calming down.

"No, I didn't know of this per se, Allōs, but I was warned by Mother. She said that you had anger in your future and to be wary of it. I honestly thought she was referring to your temper. I didn't realize that she was referring to this. I love the holy spirit and all, but she's too damn cryptic at times."

"What does this mean for me?" I got up and started smoking and pacing the room.

Gabriel slid a drink to Luke and me. "Allōs, relax. You'll be fine, I promise. Nothing is going to happen to you on my watch. Remember this, you're an Omega through and through as far as I'm concerned and nothing will change that. Tell me about this figure you saw."

I puffed on my cigarette and took a sip of alcohol. "His aura was dark and menacing, and it put me on edge. Simply looking at this figure spiked my anger."

"Ah, that is unmistakably Lucifer. But what would he want with you? Did he say anything?"

"No, he was silent. You didn't answer my question, Gabe. What does this mean for me?"

"I-I don't know, Allōs. This is foreign territory to me."

"Then who would know?"

"Mother."

"Then I shall go to her."

"I'm coming with you, babe."

"No, I'm fine."

"Babe, I'm coming with you."

"Fine. Thank you, Gabriel, this helped a lot."

Gabriel nodded. Luke and I spread our wings and opened the rightmost window and flew to the tallest mountain in the distance.

We arrived at a small plain wooden door with celestial symbols beautifully etched into it. I knocked and a pale-faced woman with deep emerald-green eyes and hair that fell to her waist answered the door. Her hair was the fieriest locks of ginger one could ever see. She was dressed in a deep blue, halter-top dress with exposed shoulders and large bell sleeves; silver stars trickled down the dress.

"Allōs, Luke, always so good to see you." Mother grabbed us and buried us in her arms. "Please come in."

I passed through the threshold and was greeted by a very

plain and spacious home carved into the mountain. It was a far cry from Heaven's futuristic theme. It was charming and cozy.

"What brings you two here this time of night?"

"Nothing good I feel."

Mother went to her kitchen and started brewing a pot of tea. "Before we get into that, how are you two?"

"For the most part we're wonderful," Luke chimed in.

"Oh, that's wonderful. I'm so glad that you two are getting along. Are you two getting along?"

"Now we are. Allōs and I finally see eye to eye."

"Did you give him a good talking to? It works like a charm – take it from me."

"Mother!"

"What? I'm just being honest. You're as stubborn as an ox at times, Allōs."

"Tell me about it." Luke rolled his eyes at me.

"How long have you two been together now?"

"We've been together for five years."

"You were sixteen when you met?"

"I knew him earlier, but we started dating at that age."

"You two are a good pair. He keeps you grounded, Allōs."

"Ironic that he's an air elemental."

"True, but he can snuff you out when you need to be."

"Damn right, babe."

I stuck my tongue out at Luke.

"How are the rest of the Omegas?"

"They're good but stressed. Something weird happened."

"Oh?"

"Yeah, a few things happened. I'm assuming that you're aware that Heaven is under attack."

"I have a bad feeling that war will be breaking out soon.

33

I just hope I'm wrong. What else happened?"

"We went to the Omni Realm to figure out what happened, but we got disconnected."

"That's not possible."

"Mother, Gabriel thought that too, but I felt it, Allōs felt it. We all did."

"Luke, that is the strangest thing I've heard. What else happened?"

"I had an interesting dream that left me with a mark."

Mother lifted her head from the stove and turned to me. "You went to Asparia?"

"Yes."

Mother poured the tea and handed Luke and me a cup each.

"That's not good. Nothing good ever comes out of that realm. It's a cursed place."

"Why is it a cursed place?"

"Allōs, it's a gateway for any ethereal being to contact you. These beings can be good, bad, or indifferent. Most of the times these beings wish ill will upon anyone who ventures in this realm. Allōs do me a favor. Anytime you fall asleep please be wary. Now, what happened to you exactly?" Mother led me by the hand and we all sat down.

"I think I was imprisoned somewhere. I broke free of my chains, but my heart was filled with hatred and rage. I killed everything in sight, and then a hooded figure approached me. We fought for a brief moment. He was unlike any opponent I've faced. He made little to no effort to dodge my attacks, then he broke my glaive. His aura was dark and menacing and it put me on edge. Looking at him spiked my anger. He then branded me with the symbol of the Omega."

"Lucifer! What does he want with you?" Mother sighed.

34

"I feared this day would come. I warned Gabriel about this and to keep your anger in check. I didn't realize that it would have led to this, and so soon."

"So you did know about this."

"My son, I see and know all things. This was in your future. However, it's not written in stone. Not yet. You can change this outcome. Take solace in that, my dear."

"I always forget that you're an oracle. But are you sure this is Lucifer's doing?"

"Oh absolutely. His aura fits that description perfectly. And he branded you there too. But why a brand? Most are tattoos. Hmm, this is all so peculiar. What could he possibly want with you? Did he say anything to you?"

"Gabriel asked the same question, but no, he remained silent the entire time. I saw nothing but a cloaked figure."

"But what does he want?"

"I'm not sure, Mother."

"Maybe he wants you in his army, babe? I don't see why he's being so tidy about this. Though I'm not familiar with his tactics, unlike Mother."

"You have a point. Lucifer is much more brash but why is he being so quiet? Luke, in total honesty, I'm unfamiliar with his tactics despite him being my child. But he wants you, Allōs. That much is clear. Luke, you might be onto something. I'll look further into this. You should rest."

"I think I've done enough resting for one night."

Mother offered us food and we had a nice family dinner for the first time in years. Mother, Luke, and I caught up with each other until the morning.

Our conversation was interrupted by a loud crack that ripped through the air.

"I'm sorry, but I have to report to the tower."

"No need to apologize, Allōs. Duty calls. You two should get going."

With a loving hug, we were out the door and back into Gabriel's chamber.

"Sorry for calling the meeting, everyone, but I have a theory about what happened that day."

I drew a cigarette from the air and lit it and lay back in my chair.

"What's your theory, Gabriel?" Michael asked.

"Michael, I know it sounds crazy, but I feel that someone was with us during that mission. That's the only explanation that I can think of. I even went back to the realm, and it was nothing on our part."

Noah raised his hand.

"What's up, Noah?"

"Luke, when I say this, I mean no disrespect..."

I leaned forward and eyed Noah.

"Al, don't worry. I'm not going to tear Luke apart."

I deeply exhaled the smoke from my nose and leaned back into my chair.

"Luke, could it have been on your end? And to be fair, it could have been myself or Allōs as well."

"I don't think so, Noah. If I had lost focus we would have come back to the void."

"That is true. Well, there goes that. Allōs, what about you?"

"I felt fairly focused, though I guess I could have lost it when we made contact. But again, we would have come to the void."

"Ariel, Raphael, did you notice anything while we were away?" Gabriel asked.

36

"The only notable thing that happened was there were reports of these half-bird half-human creatures attacking. Other than that, nothing interesting."

"Thank you, Ariel. But if they are the group I'm thinking of then I know who's leading the charge," Michael chimed in.

"Who would that be?"

"Allōs, if my memory serves me, the organization is called the Flock, which is headed by Mephistopheles."

"What would he want?"

"I don't know, Gabe. Maybe to create chaos? That is what he's known for."

"You have a point, Michael. It's possible."

We continued theorizing about what could have happened that day. Something didn't feel right about the room. The room felt hotter than normal. I couldn't place it, but I felt a massive energy signature within these walls. It felt raw and unclean; it wasn't the kind of energy I've felt before. I felt the energy surge and the temperature started to spike rapidly.

"Everyone get down!" Snapping my fingers, I encased all of us in a thin halo of blue that acted like an impenetrable armor. Then we were all engulfed in a fiery inferno and thrown miles away from the tower like rag dolls. I went flying out of the window in a wave of glass and fire. I quickly enabled my armor by tapping my chest. A thick black liquid formed all over my body and then hardened while I lost all sense of sound and sight.

I landed in the town square and had the wind knocked out of me as I rolled for a good distance before stopping. My entire body hurt. I tried getting up and immediately fell to the ground. I summoned my glaive and propped myself up and walked down the street trying to catch my breath. Keeping my encasement spell was an undertaking, for I was too weak and I needed to be healed.

I limped the streets looking for the Omegas, hoping that they had landed nearby. I couldn't find anyone and the streets were oddly quiet. Everything was burned to a crisp; so many homes were destroyed. I was able to get the entire scale of the damage from last night. Specks of yellow light were littered about in the distance. I tapped my forehead and the armor encased my head. I summoned six more copies of my weapon for them to float about me. I heard something running across the roofs of the houses. I whipped my head around and saw nothing. I spread my wings and flew above the rooflines and saw nothing. I gently placed myself on the ground and continued to struggle as I walked down the streets.

A dark ominous cackle boomed around me.

"Lucifer, show yourself." My glaives surrounded me, pointing outward. Ahead, a demon in crimson armor appeared in front of me.

"You flatter me, Allōs, but I'm afraid that I'm not the one you're looking for."

A towering giant of a demon, seven feet tall, with gray skin and large ram horns, stood before me. I remembered this demon well – how could I forget? He was the living proof of my greatest failure as an Omega.

"Arzon the Conqueror."

"So you remember me?"

"Of course. Your crimson armor is unforgettable, not to mention you are the result of my greatest failure."

"Ah, those pathetic excuses for archangels! Gabriel must be slipping, letting any runt join the mighty Omegas. I forgot what their names were again. Please regale me," he said, as he spat on the street. I stayed silent. "Go on, tell me, Allōs the Blue, eighth archangel of the Omegas, the mighty executioner. Tell me!"

I gritted my teeth and said, "Abigail the Jade, Zachary the Sapphire and Alexandria the Ivory."

"Very good! Now was that so hard?" With a flourish of his hand, a battle axe appeared in his left hand. It was a massive double-headed blade with wickedly serrated edges that would tear through flesh mercilessly. Hoisting it over his shoulder, he just stood there idly waiting.

I said, "What business do you have here?"

"I'm here to enjoy the chaos, to do a little bit of conquering and killing. You know, the usual."

Arzon uttered that statement with such casual callousness I swelled up with anger and launched a glaive straight into one of his seven hearts. "You!" I exclaimed. "You set off the bomb in Gabriel's chambers, didn't you?!"

Arzon struggled to speak.

"If...I had the chance to kill the mighty Gabriel...I would, but not with a bomb! That is the weapon of a coward!"

While I was in shock at what I had heard, he brutally hammered my chest with his axe, ripping into my chest. I stumbled to my feet, hunched over, trying to keep the blood from dripping onto the street. The glaives that circled me came to the front of me and pointed at Arzon. I whipped my arm upward and a large stone cross jumped from beneath the ground behind Arzon. I pushed my hand forward and swiped fingers to the right which bolted Arzon to the cross ready to be crucified. The glaives moved away from me as I stepped forward.

"If you weren't the one who bombed the Omegas, then which demon did?"

"Who's to say it was a demon who bombed your precious Omegas?"

I was completely taken aback by that statement and I

floundered, trying to think of what to say. "Of…of course it was a demon. Who else would have a vendetta against the angels?"

"There might be a being that hates your kind even more than us."

"Doubtful." I sent six other glaives plunging into Arzon's hearts. He began to chuckle masochistically. The chuckle grew in volume until it peaked into a roaring guffaw. He ripped the glaives from his chest and himself from the cross, picking up his axe before slamming it into my chest once more. It tore my armor from shoulder to hip and broke through my fire barrier like nothing. I jumped back, leaving a trail of blood in my path. I had my weapons form a wall between me and him; they bristled with anticipation. My armor shifted itself together, hardening and mending its gaping wound.

Arzon gleefully charged me as I multiplied my weapons from seven to fifty. He hacked recklessly through waves of them as I stood behind them, watching in panic. Then he reached for me as he came closer, brandishing his mighty axe with more fervor. Only five glaives stood…

I unleashed a wall of hellfire, hitting Arzon's face. This drove him backward violently into the cross behind him. His shrieks were heard around the neighborhood mixed with the clang of his dropped axe. My blue flames encircled his wrists like snakes slithering up his arms, binding him to the cross again. I flicked my finger forward, inching my weapons into Arzon's hearts, causing another wail of agony.

I said, "On the precipice of death it is customary to allow the condemned to speak their final thoughts."

"Allōs…everything we demons do is just and righteous," Arzon coughed, "while everything you angels do is evil in the eyes of our kind."

40

I was shocked by that statement. I never really thought about it like that, being viewed as evil.

"Now, be one with God the Father, the Son, and the Holy Spirit," I said, as I signed the cross in the air. Then I whipped my hand upward. A small blue orb of light emitted from the center of his chest, growing rapidly larger until the searing flames engulfed him, the cross, and the street touching the cross, obliterating him from existence forever. The only evidence that was left of his existence was his axe, armor, and the scorch mark on the street.

As the orb decreased, I said to myself, *I should probably let the others know where I am.* Almost as an afterthought, I flicked my finger, sending the orb rocketing upward until it exploded into a bright blue rain, covering the skyline in a dazzling array. Out of curiosity, I attempted to pick up Arzon's axe. *Holy shit it's heavy.* I winced in pain. *Why did I expect it to be lighter? It is a magnificent weapon, I'll give him that.* I limped down the street, fighting the urge to fall.

The pain in my chest subsided, but it was still noticeably there. I was still shaken by the whole thing. *What's going on? If a demon didn't set off the bomb then who did? One of us? No, that can't be right. No one would ever betray us like that. It's more than likely Mephisto. What did we do to deserve this? Are we the evil ones? Of course not, Allōs, why would you say that? I serve God, the most just being in the universe.*

"Allōs!"

I whipped my head around to see an angel all in white barreling toward me and before I knew it I was in someone's arms on the ground.

"Fuck, that hurt! Will you watch where you're going?"

"I'm so glad you survived! I was worried sick!"

I paused to understand what was happening. "Luke?"

41

"Who else would it be? What happened to you? Why is it whenever I leave you alone you get some form of injury?" Luke hugged me and healed my injuries. He has always been the one to show the most affection toward anyone out of all of us. I usually don't have a problem with it unless it's while we are on duty, but I push through it.

"How did you find me?"

"Easy. I saw the blue rain and I knew it was you. Not to mention the cross." Luke tapped my forehead and the armor receded into the neckline. "There you are. I hate these face masks. They're so restricting and I feel like I can't breathe. Plus, I don't get to see your cute face."

I rolled my eyes. "Luke, you can be such a dork sometimes."

"I know. Your point?"

"That you're a dork. Now help me up."

"Of course." Luke flapped his wings and got us on our feet. Luke brushed the dust off me. A column of shimmering light descended from the sky onto our position, revealing itself to be none other than Gabriel in his gleaming golden armor.

A small crowd began to form around us as people were clamoring with excitement to see all of us together.

"Is that Gabriel the Gold?"

"Look, it's Allōs the Blue!"

"It's Luke the White!"

The rest of the Omegas found their way to us and the crowd became more star-struck.

"Jophiel the Auburn, I love you," a voice exclaimed, swarming up from the cacophony.

"I love you too," she responded in a kind and loving voice.

The archangels are known celebrities along with the others that reside within Heaven. We are usually busy with our allotted

42

duties so we are rarely seen all together. However, we are widely known for everything that we do, mostly our military and charity work. To everyone we are known as the protector, thus we are put on a proverbial pedestal, making us famous. It can grate on my nerves at times like these when it gets in the way of our work since I'm here to protect and *not* be famous. Doing as Gabriel always taught me, I just smiled and waved.

"Allōs, I see that you found Luke."

"Rather he found me. It's good to see that all of you were unharmed, especially you, Gabe."

Gabriel ruffled my hair. "Omegas, we must head to the war room before things get more out of hand."

43

Chapter 3

"Gabriel, is it really that urgent?"

"Unfortunately so, Jophiel, more than we realized. We don't have time to waste."

Why the war room? What even is the war room and why is it so bad?

"Gabriel, what is the war room?"

"It's a room for war, Al," Luke interjected.

"What? I never would have guessed! Thanks for clearing that up, babe. I know that much, Luke, but why is everyone freaking about it?"

"We sealed off that room after the Luciferian wars and swore that none of the original seven would ever open those cursed doors again," Ariel answered.

We spread our wings and rocketed our way westward away from civilization and arrived in the heart of a mountain. We glided to a halt in front of massive double doors that stood fifty feet tall with effigies of the original seven Omegas imprinted on them.

"Why is Michael first? I know this is the chain of command – was Michael in command at one point?"

"Yes, Allōs, I was in command for a time. After the Luciferian wars I gave the position to Gabriel."

"Couldn't handle the pressure, buddy?"

"Oh for sure. All of you are so demanding so I gave you the distinct honor of carrying our load," Michael said, as he placed his hand on Gabriel's shoulder.

"Anyway, Allōs, open the doors please."

Upon closer inspection, there was an indentation in the door at eye level, which was revealed to be the shape of a hand with a hole about the size of a golf ball resting in its palm.

"What is this place?" Luke inquired, as he cast his eyes all over the doors, never staying in one spot for too long.

"Are you going to inquire about every little thing?" Noah huffed, closing his eyes and pinching the bridge of his nose.

I started feeling that boiling rage in my heart again.

"Ease up! He was only inducted a month ago," I barked harshly, as I felt my eyes sting then subside.

"I've never seen you do that before."

"Do what?"

"Your eyes flashed blue. Usually they flash white when you're mad."

"That's the second time that I've seen it happen, Noah."

"Huh, interesting, Gabriel."

"To answer your question, Luke, this is the room where we oversaw the Luciferian War, after which I had this room sealed off. After we shut down this forsaken place, everyone prayed it would never come into use again. Though, unfortunately, here we all are." Ariel ran her hand across the cold steel doors as memories of the war flooded her mind, causing tears to start running across her alabaster skin as her raven hair draped in front of her eyes. She brushed her hair out of her eyes and said, "After this war, I hope to never see these doors ever again." She sniffed quietly, fighting back more tears.

I tried to reach out and comfort her, but she stopped me.

"I'm fine, Allōs." She smiled through her tears and continued, "Thank you, dear, you're very sweet for wanting to help." Gently placing her forehead against the steel doors, she composed herself, and taking a deep breath she said, "Gabriel, Michael, if you bring me here ever again I will destroy this very mountain. Do I make myself clear?" Her gaze pierced through Gabriel.

"Absolutely, Ariel, it wasn't my wish to upset you so."

"Good. Now that we are on the same page…"

"How do we get inside?" I asked. After uttering those words a tense silence broke and restlessness replaced it.

Ariel motioned me forward. "If you would do the honors. Simply place your hand in the slot and blast as much fire into it as you can to make our eyes glow the color of your flames. Then we can get inside."

"How will I know when to stop?"

"Just make the eyes glow and I'll guide you."

I approached the door, hesitating before placing my hand in the slot. After taking a deep breath, I exhaled and pushed as much of the fire from my palm as I could.

"One." It seemed like minutes until she counted to two and only seemed like moments before the numbers climbed to five.

"Seven." No sooner did she utter the number than the ground shifted so violently that I hovered above it to keep myself from falling as the doors split open.

"I like blue more than yellow."

"What's wrong with yellow?" Gabriel asked.

"Oh nothing. I just like seeing blue eyes for a change." I gently landed and walked through the entrance. The doors slid behind us shaking the ground once more as the sound echoed through the hall.

I said, "Question, Ariel."

"Hmm?"

"If Gabriel is also a fire elemental, why didn't he open the door? Doesn't he possess more power than I do?"

"Yes, but we all swore never to open that door again. Unfortunately, we all have to open another set of doors. Ugh, I hate this place," she said, as she walked toward the next set of doors, her footsteps echoing through the hall. I nodded in understanding, wondering if I would've had the same strength to face this like Ariel did. We proceeded down an immense hall with soaring columns leading toward a singular massive door across the corridor. As we got closer, seven handprints like the one on the outside door lay before us embedded on this set of doors. Ariel, Azrael, Chamuel, Gabriel, Jophiel, Michael, and Raphael gathered stoically in front of the door, where they placed their hands, pushing inward on the metal and unlocking the door. The doors creaked open which gave off a horrible sound of the metal hinges squeaking against each other.

Inside was a large oval table with seven chairs gathered around it, covered in years' worth of dust. Chamuel gently started swirling his hand and the dust started to swirl around the room and into three vents hidden in the ceiling, which rejuvenated the room.

There were many things lying about as if the Omegas had got up and left without notice. Maps were strewn about haphazardly, while ashtrays had been left unattended and half-opened liquor bottles were strewn on the shelves. I quietly looked about the shelves and noticed that the liquor bottles were from The Empty Oak, a very popular tavern just outside of the town square.

"I'm sorry, Natalie," I said under my breath.

"Who's Natalie?" Ariel asked.

I nearly jumped out of my skin and tried not to break any of the bottles on the shelf.

"She was a friend. However, she lost her way and I had to do something that I'm not proud of. I suppose that is the curse of being an Omega at times."

Ariel turned me around and saw my tortured expression. She held both of my hands and said, "Allōs, that is the grim reality of being an Omega. We have all had to kill our fallen friends and it has always rattled us to the core. I lost a sister at the beginning of the Luciferian wars just as you lost Natalie."

"You had to kill her?"

"I did. Allōs, my dear, remember this – you did the right thing. Just forgive yourself, love. Do you want a hug?"

"I would like one very much." Ariel gave me a loving hug and assured me that everything was going to be alright.

"How long has it been, Ariel?"

She turned and met the gaze of Raphael. "Thousands of years, my friend."

"Not long enough," Raphael stated morosely.

"Gather round," Gabriel said quietly, gesturing at us to sit. The original seven took their places at the table leaving Noah, Luke, and me to stand hovering nearby. "Allōs, first and foremost, I want to say thank you for saving us. Without your quick thinking we wouldn't be alive and for that we are all in your debt."

Everyone bowed their heads to me. It was an odd sensation to be bowed to. I get where Gabriel comes from now when he tells me not to. I bowed back to show my thanks then we swiftly continued our meeting.

"It's no secret that a war is brewing," Gabriel continued. "I feel that the second demon war is at our doorstep. I have a hunch that it will start here near the northern mountain range. This war will be something that we haven't seen before. This doesn't seem like it's Lucifer leading the helm. It's too sloppy for his taste. I feel that the initial attack was planned by him, but after that the plan fell apart. It's too reckless."

"It could be Mephistopheles. It sounds like his antics."

"I was thinking that, Michael, and I have a good feeling that it might be him. He's always wanted to impress Lucifer by creating chaos, however to no avail."

"What about the figure we saw in the archives?"

"Great question, Luke, but the only thing that makes sense for me is that Mephisto probably disconnected us. He's sloppy but not stupid. If he had a brain, he would have removed that figure that Allōs contacted."

"You can do that?"

"Believe it or not, Allōs, you can. However, it takes a very powerful person to do that. There's only three people that I know of that have such power to figure it out. Those being the son of God, Jesus, the holy spirit, Loreley, and God himself."

Mother's name is Loreley? How come I never knew that? I pulled a cigarette out of my pocket and proceeded to light it to stave off the quiet.

"Allōs, can you spare a cigarette?" Ariel asked.

I was incredibly shocked by that request. I had always thought of Ariel being more virtuous than myself or Gabriel.

"Actually a cigarette sounds amazing," Jophiel chimed in.

"I could use one," Michael said.

"Michael, you smoke?"

"Pick up your jaw from the floor. But yes I do on occasion."

"Huh, who knew." I gave Ariel the pack. She picked out a cigarette and passed it to Jophiel who passed it to Michael.

49

I sent a small pulse of fire around the table to light their smokes. Ariel inhaled then exhaled and a cloud of smoke streamed out of her mouth. The room started to fill with a thin veil of smoke that rolled around the air.

"Thanks, dear."

"No problem, Ariel."

"Yes, thank you, Allōs," Michael said.

Jophiel blew a kiss at me from across the room.

Gabriel snapped his fingers and ten golden goblets and a simple decanter full of wine appeared on the table. The decanter began to quickly pour its contents into each goblet, filling each one, and then gently set itself on the table. Everyone took a goblet as Noah brought mine over.

"Thanks, man."

"No problem, mate."

"Oh, sorry for snapping at you. I always hate yelling at people, especially at any of you."

"Don't worry about it, Al. You're fine."

"To Allōs!" everyone said, raising their glasses.

"Cheers." Noah and I bumped our glasses together then took a sip of wine.

Gabriel said, "I need all of us to be in this together, acting as an absolute unit, if we are going to win this. Don't worry, we have the entire army of Heaven backing us, but we need to stick together."

"How long do we have, Gabe?" Michael asked, as a plume of smoke drifted from his mouth.

"According to the timeline, half a year give or take, till the entire army starts its marching on our soil. But I have a feeling that they will start attacking the northern mountain range in a few days."

"Who's leading the attack? Mephisto?"

"I wish I knew, Luke. However, more than likely it would be him."

"What does Lucifer have to do with this then, Gabe?"

"Azrael, that's a very good question. He's the coordinator, but I doubt that he's heavily involved. I genuinely believe the only reason he's involved was to map out Heaven for Mephisto."

I took a sip of my wine and it burned on the way down, making me cough. *A bit strong for wine*, I thought.

"We can't be certain about anything. We have to send someone for intel. Until then it's only speculation. Everything alright, Al?"

"Yeah, Gabe, it just went down the windpipe. Ignore me." I waved my hand in dismissal. Everyone looked away. "All of you can fuck right off." They all giggled at my expense. I smiled and took a drag and exhaled.

"What does this mean for Heaven and for us?" Noah asked.

"For Heaven, it means that we prepare for war once again. For us, Noah, it means nothing and no matter what happens to us, we stand together and we die together. You have my word."

"Do you think that Allōs, Luke and I are ready?"

"Yes, there's not a doubt in my mind. You three are the perfect team. Noah, you are an excellent strategist. Luke, you are a gifted healer and, Allōs, your fighting abilities are unprecedented. You three are worthy Omegas. You have nothing to fear." Gabriel raised his glass again in another toast. "To the Omegas!"

"To the Omegas!"

"Let's take in these last moments of peace we have before this war falls upon us by enjoying a nice feast together." With a snap of his fingers, Gabriel had the table instantly covered in platters of every kind of food. We each took a plate and enjoyed our company as usual, but we couldn't help but feel a sense of dread looming over us.

I robotically filled my plate, not concentrating much on what was there or what I was eating and I grew quiet as I took a place at the table along with Luke and Noah. Multiple things were running through my head at the speed of light.

Memories of Natalie turning replayed in my head. *"Crucify me!"* she screamed. This scene played in my head as if it were stuck on a loop. I felt myself start to spiral.

"Everything's going to be alright, Allōs. It's Natalie, isn't it?"

I smiled wanly back at Gabriel. "Yeah."

"Al."

"What's up, Michael?"

"The deepest solace lies in understanding, and we all have endured the agonizing pain you are feeling. Always remember that we understand more than anyone. Isn't that right, everyone?"

"Absolutely," Jophiel replied.

"Of course." Gabriel nodded.

"Sure." Noah shrugged.

"Most definitely." Raphael raised his cup to me.

"No doubt." Azrael balled up his napkin and threw it at me.

"Without a thought." Ariel gave a winning smile.

"Of course, babe." Luke beamed.

"Obviously." Chamuel rolled his eyes.

"Thanks, everyone."

"Of course, Allōs. That's what we're here for. We are a family after all," Michael said.

I felt a sharp twinge in my stomach and on my chest as my body contorted in pain.

"Allōs, are you alright?" Jophiel looked worried and like she was about to get up. Just as quickly as it had happened, it subsided and I felt normal again.

"Yeah, I feel fine. Must've been nothing." I smiled reassuringly at her, picked my utensils up, and continued to eat.

Time passed while we made conversation, trying to make the best of this situation. Then I felt a searing pain on my chest.

"Al, what's that on your chest?"

I looked down and saw that my brand was glowing proudly through my shirt. "I can explain, Ariel," I said in a panic. I felt myself shaking in fear. *Fuck, fuck, fuck.*

"It looks like it's a seal of some sort," Jophiel chimed in.

"Everyone, I can explain! I got it during a dream!" I felt myself backing away from the others. Gabriel stood up from the table in an attempt to console me. In a quick, panicked motion nine glaives leaped from the floor and were at everyone's throats. I looked around and couldn't believe that I had just drawn my weapons at my own family. I was horrified, but I couldn't move. I was frozen in fear. I wanted to run away, I was so ashamed of myself.

"Please don't come any closer."

"Allōs, it's us. We love you. We would never want to hurt you."

"*Kill them!*" barked a deep voice from the back of my head.

I shook my head and continued backing up till I was startled when I hit a wall. "Kill them!" the voice screamed.

"No! Get out of my head! I won't kill them!"

"*Kill them!*"

"No! I won't!" I said, as I felt embers start to form around me.

"Allōs, lay down your weapons!" Michael barked.

"Give me one good reason why I should! You're going to kill me when I do! I beg you, please don't kill me!"

"Michael! You're scaring him! Can't you tell he's terrified?" Jophiel scolded.

"You're talking to me like I'm some kind of untamed animal."

"Allōs, you're not an animal. We all know that," Jophiel said.

"Allōs, why would I kill you?"

"Because, Michael, of what I had to do to Natalie, and there's this voice…" I said, as I inched my glaive closer to Michael's throat.

"Voice? What voice?"

"I heard this voice telling me to kill her. I ignored it as best I could, but now it's back with a vengeance telling me to kill you."

"Allōs, slow down. You're talking fast. What's going on?" Luke asked.

"Please, just tell me everything's going to be okay."

"Babe, everything is going to be fine."

I looked around the room and everyone looked back at me with a concerned look. I let my glaives fade into the ether, and slid to the floor and turned away. Tears started to run down my face as I felt someone hug me from behind. I looked back and saw Luke.

"Don't look at me. I'm too ashamed to face all of you, especially you, Luke," I said, covering my face.

Luke put my hand down and grabbed the sides of my face and locked eyes with me.

"No, please don't look at me."

"Why? I love those beautiful green eyes of yours."

I got up and gathered myself as much as I could. "Everyone, I'm so sorry for threatening you. This wasn't what I wanted. I was going to tell you what happened, but not like this. I'm not a killer. I promise I would never willingly hur—" Then my stomach pain came slamming into me from out of nowhere, stomach pains so unbelievably unbearable. I crumpled into myself and rolled onto my back writhing in pain as I started violently vomiting.

"Prop him up!" Noah yelled.

The group came rushing to my side and helped prop me against the wall. Luke started cleaning me up with a napkin. I only had a moment of reprieve after I stopped vomiting. Luke held me tight in his arms and didn't let go. I started to feel at peace. I felt myself getting heavier and I started leaning forward.

"Al, you okay?"

I tried to say something, but Luke didn't seem to respond. I tried saying his name; he didn't respond.

"Allōs, stay with me!"

All I could do was stare at him mutely. Luke's face started to lose color and my vision started shifting in and out. I was cold. I tried calling out, but no one heard me.

"Allōs!" Luke was screaming my name as my eyes rolled back into my head before I lost consciousness...

"What the hell just happened?"

"Nothing, Noah. Allōs threw up and decided to take a nap. What the fuck do you think?"

"Luke, I know you're upset. Just help me rationalize what happened."

"I'm trying to do that myself! I...I don't know what happened, Noah, okay!"

"Could it be something he ate?" Michael quickly scanned the table, looking for anything that looked out of place.

"It could've been something he drank," Ariel volunteered.

"It could've been either of those things. Jophiel, did you see anything, any telltale signs?"

"Nothing you guys didn't see."

Tears of frustration started to fall as I placed my hands on Allōs's chest. His body arched off the floor as my healing encased him in a shroud of white.

"Wake up, wake up. *Please* wake up, Al," I continued muttering to myself, as my magic searched for something, anything, it could heal. Everyone held their breath as they all waited for a verdict, knowing there was nothing I couldn't fix. The white shroud dissipated from Allōs's form and no notable change presented itself.

"I don't understand. There's no reading." I cast my spell again, putting a bit more force into it, but once more there was no notable change. I was about ready to break down as I motioned for Michael to join Allōs at my side. I placed my hands over Michael's and we both pushed their combined healing into Allōs, but nothing changed.

"Why isn't it working!?" I raged, as tears streamed down my face. I looked at Michael imploringly.

"Could you sense anything about his condition? Why couldn't he be healed?"

"His soul is being attacked. Notice how his mark is glowing. It'll stop when his transformation is complete."

"He's turning?"

"I don't know. I've never seen this before. Usually their eyes turn black, they get a tattoo and that's the end of it. But Allōs's case is a strange one."

"Can we fix it?"

"I don't think so. We have to let it play out. I can sense his soul crying out for help. Allōs is desperately clinging on to life as darkness tries to silence him. Surely you must have sensed that."

"I did, Michael. He's calling out for help but no one can hear him. Is he dying?" I could barely choke out the words.

"No, but he is changing."

I felt my face crumple more in despair. "Can it be reversed?"

"Only because he's an archangel, yes. However, it will be a difficult undertaking for him. He does have much anger in him and that is what demons glom onto. So he has to fight it himself, only if he wants to."

"He might not want to fight when he wakes up."

Michael pulled me into his arms and held on tight. "Hush now, Luke. I have no doubt that he will want to reverse this. He wants to fight this. He didn't kill us, did he? Everything is going to be absolutely fine, Luke. I know it doesn't seem like it, but I promise it will all work out for both of you."

"You have a point."

"Now, go clean yourself up. We have to make a visit to the family."

"Where are we taking him?"

"Well, we can't fix him, but I know someone who can. Plus, it's a safe place to keep him from the war…our mother."

Chapter 4

The Omegas carried Allōs to Mother's house and upon arrival gave a somber knock on the door. Mother was shocked to see us all.

"Michael, so good to see you. What's wrong with Allōs? Please come inside. I have tea ready."

"Mother, where should I put Allōs?"

"Put him on the sofa, Luke."

"Mother, I believe that Allōs is in the midst of a transformation."

She rushed over to him and noticed that his chest was glowing. "This isn't good. Everyone gather round. Let me show you something." Everyone huddled around Mother as she surrounded her hand in energy. She ran her finger from Allōs's forehead to his chest. The moment she touched his chest she recoiled her hand.

"Huh," Mother said.

"What's wrong, Mother?" I asked.

"Something isn't accepting my energy. It's more than likely whatever is possessing Allōs at the moment."

"Allōs is being possessed?"

"To me it feels that he's being held hostage."

Gabriel asked, "How is he being held hostage?"

"Well if you noticed when I touched his chest, a surge of

58

energy went through my hand. That's an anti-magic spell. Something doesn't want me to get in." Mother sighed. "Everyone, this isn't your normal transformation by any means. He is in great pain. His soul is essentially tearing itself apart. He's in constant turmoil with his thoughts and emotions."

"That would explain why he lashed out at us so violently."

"What did he do, Gabriel?" Mother said sharply.

"He thought we were going to kill him because of his situation, to the point where he was ready to kill us. He was yelling out that he wouldn't kill us. I'm assuming he was yelling at the voice in his head."

"Oh, it's worse than I thought. Let's see if this works." Mother went to her nearest closet and took out a golden shawl made of fleece and draped it over Allōs. "Hopefully this should help."

Michael asked, "You're sure it will work?"

"To be honest, Michael, I wouldn't know. I don't think anything will come from this, but it's worth a try."

As Mother draped her shawl over Allōs, his body became enveloped in a healing amber light. Mother studied Allōs's mark intensely, hoping that the light would fade. However, nothing happened. She sighed. "Perhaps this will ease the pain." Mother placed her hand on the right side of Allōs's chest. Her hand started to glow and when she lifted her hand a series of dots rested on his shirt. Upon further inspection these dots made a pattern. The pattern fell through his shirt and down onto his skin and then the light faded. Mother watched the right side of his chest and his brand's light grew dull and then started glowing again. Mother sighed.

"Mother, what did you mark him with?"

"The Ophiuchus constellation, Luke."

"Why that constellation in particular?"

"This constellation is said to hold some healing properties. And judging how his brand reacted, it worked. But barely." Mother looked down at Allōs. "I'm sorry, Allōs, there is nothing more I can do now. This is in your hands. I trust that you will do the right thing."

The imminent war broke out, and weeks passed as it raged across the plains of Heaven, while Allōs lay motionless in Mother's home. The Omegas and I took turns keeping Allōs company when we had the time. I had been at his side for a few days, checking up on him. I was worried sick about his condition. We had all been worried about Allōs; he had been unconscious for a few months now, with no sign of improvement. If I was being honest, I was beginning to lose hope. I couldn't bear the thought of losing my soulmate.

I opened my eyes hoping to see Mother or one of the Omegas, but the only thing around me was darkness. I felt as if I was floating; I had no bearings whatsoever. I saw something in the distance, a small blue light. The light grew larger and started to take the form of a person. From out of that light stepped a figure made of shadow. The figure's eyes were glowing a fiery blue and it had the same illuminated seal on its chest that I bore. It slowly approached me.

"Welcome, child, I trust you're comfortable." The figure spoke with a dark and sepulchral voice.

"Do I know you?"

"Allōs, you wound me. You don't recognize me?"

"Am I supposed to?"

"Why, yes. I am your guilt. I am your disquietude. I am your indifference."

"So you're my personal demon?"

"Essentially."

"Do all angels have whatever you are inside them?"

"No. Only a few have them but those who did, you killed."

"Then I shall kill you as well."

This creature erupted in a loud guffaw. "You can't kill me! However, I can kill you!"

"What do you mean?"

"You'll understand soon enough, Allōs."

"Who are you?"

The figure wrapped itself around me and placed its shadowy hands on my shoulders and whispered, "I am the voice that you use to speak against your conscience."

"You! You're the one telling me to kill."

The figure gave me a wicked smile. "Good. Good, now you understand."

"Where am I?"

"Sêle Asparia." The figure danced around me as I followed its motion.

"The realm of the soul?"

"Good, Allōs. And what does this realm do that separates it from Sueniros Asparia?"

"I wouldn't know."

"I would expect a highly educated angel such as yourself to know his surroundings. I can't blame you though. It's not a place that the angels would inform you about. The truth be told about this place, it's a plain where we demons lurk. But Sueniros is a bit different. That is the dream realm – I will be communicating with you there from this moment onward. I don't have many angels come to the realm of the soul. However, if they do, they will be faced with a test."

"A test?"

The figure grabbed me by the throat and squeezed hard. I coughed as I tried to breathe. I felt myself getting lightheaded.

"Yes, and this test will make you crumble if I have anything to say about it."

He then dropped me and I caught my breath. I gasped for air. I looked down and saw that something was glowing on the right side of my chest. Pulled on the collar of my shirt and looked in and saw a constellation. I smiled; I knew that this was Mother's handiwork. I didn't know what she wanted me to do though. I touched the right side of my chest and I looked at my hand and saw the constellation resting in the palm of my left hand. I got back up to my feet.

"I feel like it's a bit unfair that you know my name and I don't know yours," I said as I started backing away slowly.

"My name is Ovelth, king of the Xorraths."

"What is a Xorrath?" I continued to back away till I hit a wall. I placed my left hand on the wall hoping that the constellation would transfer to it. A few moments later I could feel a slight presence of magic behind me.

"A Xorrath is a demon of the mind. We lurk deep inside your soul."

"Do you serve Lucifer?"

"No! I am deeply offended that you would ask such a question. I came long before Lucifer!"

The being shifted into a spectral form with a flowing tail, brandishing two grotesquely long arms with bony claw-like fingers. Ram horns haloed him as they twirled off in opposite directions, accentuating the dragon shape of his head; his steely gaze never left my own.

"Allōs, do you really think that an ethereal marking will stop me?"

He grew rapidly larger, gaining in momentous size as his blazing blue eyes stared me down before he swallowed me whole.

"Allōs, I know you can hear me. I miss you, we all do. I want you to hug me again and tell me everything will be alright. Wake up, please, for me. I hope you pull through. It's been three months now and to be honest, Al, I'm beginning to lose hope."

Mother entered the room and said, "Luke, my son, never lose hope! Hope is what keeps us going."

"I know. It's just so hard."

I noticed that Allōs's left side of his chest was glowing. "Mother, I think you should see this."

"What's wrong, Luke?"

"Is his left side tattoo supposed to be glowing?"

"No, it is not." Mother placed her hand on Allōs's forehead and slid it down to his chest. She smiled. "I don't know what he did, but he gave us a way in."

"What do you mean by that?"

"Well, Luke, his body is accepting my energy now. Like I said I don't know what he did to grant us access, but I knew that he would pull through."

"What now, Mother?"

"We go and get him."

I looked down and noticed that my ring was blinking.

"Is that supposed to happen?" Mother asked.

"Oh this, yeah. It's how we keep in contact with each other."

"I don't have one of those. I should get one."

"You should, Mother. We could talk more often then." I tapped my diamond ring and a ghostly image of Gabriel appeared.

"Luke, I need you back."

Mother chimed in, "Sorry, Gabriel, I need Luke to pull Allōs out of his coma."

"I thought you said that would kill him if you tried."

"Yes, but he gave us a way in."

"Mother, I need Luke though."

"Gabriel, don't argue with me. I need Luke so that Allōs sees a familiar face when he wakes up."

"Alright, Mother, you win this round. Luke, report back after Allōs has settled in."

"Yes, sir."

"Oh, Gabriel, when will you let me lead the Omegas?" Mother asked.

"Whenever you would like. We could use you – you're a phenomenal leader, Mother, we could really use you."

"I'm flattered, Gabriel. Not to mention that my armor needs a good dusting. I will see you in the fray." Gabriel's image faded away into my ring. Mother turned to Allōs.

"Luke, let's see what's really at play here."

Chapter 5

Mother gently placed the back of her palm on his forehead and dragged it across his head. A dark cloud followed her motions as she circled her wrist, and the room was completely shrouded in darkness.

"Mother, what's going on?"

"You'll see. Take my hand." I took Mother's hand and we started walking into darkness. We kept walking until we were stopped at a cathedral door with runes sloppily scratched onto the surface.

"Mother, what language is this?"

"It's Xorrathian, the language of the Xorraths."

"What does it say?"

"It spells *Sêle Asparia*." This place was cold. I felt myself begin to shake. I touched the doors and I felt a powerful shock go through my body; my arm went numb.

"Mother, what is this place?"

"Luke, this is Sêle Asparia, or the realm of the soul. It's a place where demons exist. And judging by the size of this place, Ovelth has been here for a while now. Allōs, what happened to you?" Mother asked. With a flick of her wrist the doors obediently flew open, and we stepped through the threshold. Inside was a long hallway with reflective walls with creatures clawing at the surface trying desperately to escape.

"What are those? Are those Allōs's demons? Why are there so many of them?"

"No need to be afraid, Luke."

"I am though."

"Don't worry, Luke. These demons can't get us."

"Step forth, Loreley," beckoned a voice that resonated through the hallway.

"If this is your attempt to scare me, then be gone with you." With a casual flick of a fireball at the walls, which burst into flames, we made our way through the hall until we were greeted by yet another door.

"I knew your soul was being torn apart by these creatures. Al, please stay strong and whatever you do, don't let them consume you," Mother said. The door ahead opened and we entered a dark void of a room.

"Loreley, pleased to make your acquaintance once more. And this must be Luke," Ovelth said as he circled around me.

"Hello, Ovelth. What do you want with Allōs?" I asked.

"To watch him tear himself apart!" he said as he floated to the middle of the room.

"Not if I have anything to say about it!" Mother exclaimed.

"I look forward to it!" Ovelth said, as he pulled Allōs from the shadows and threw him at us. I caught him in my arms and Ovelth laughed and faded away, leaving only us. Allōs groaned and opened his eyes.

"Luke, what are you doing here?"

"Getting you out of here, babe. Let's go home. Get some rest if you can." Allōs held on to me as I followed Mother as we re-entered her home. I placed Allōs on the couch and sat next to him. Allōs's brand finally stopped glowing. He phased back into reality and looked deep into my eyes and smiled. He hugged me tight and kissed me gently.

"Hey babe, thanks for bringing me out of my coma."

"Thank Mother. She was the one who brought you out."

"Thank you, Mother."

"You're quite welcome, Allōs. It's good to have you back," she said as she hugged him. She then went to the kitchen and grabbed a tea pot and two cups. She then poured Allōs and me a cup of tea.

"It's nice to be back, Mother." With three fingers he grabbed the air and pulled a cigarette into existence. "Do you mind, Mother?" Mother sighed.

"Only this once." She placed an ashtray on the table in front of the sofa.

He snapped his fingers, but nothing happened. "What?"

"Huh, you lost your powers. Fascinating. Don't worry, Al. My sister will help you with that."

"You have a sister, Mother?"

"Yes, but we haven't spoken in years."

Allōs tossed his cigarette into the ashtray and sipped his tea. "What happened? I had my powers a few days ago."

"Actually, Al, you've been out for three months," I said.

"What of the war?"

"Everything is stable at the moment, Al. The Omegas are making good progress on the northern front. Everything should level out soon."

"I just wish I was there, Luke." Allōs sighed. "Mother, I need to get something off of my chest."

"What's wrong, Allōs?"

"I did something I'm not proud of."

"And what was that?"

Allōs gently held my hand and then sighed. "I threatened my family. Not only that, but I was prepared to kill them."

"Why is that, Allōs?"

"We were in the war room and my brand started to shine through my shirt. Ariel noticed it and I panicked. I don't know why I thought this, but I believed that they were going to kill me because I was turning. Mother, Luke, I hate myself for that. I'm so sorry."

"Babe, I forgive you."

"I know, thank you, babe."

"Allōs, no need to apologize to me, apologize to the Omegas."

"I'll be sure to. Mother, what does this mean for me?"

Mother fell silent and looked into her tea.

"I don't know, Allōs. However, I have a feeling I know where you are headed."

"Where would that be?"

"Nowhere good, I feel. You're turning. I don't know if you're turning into a demon, but a demonic side of you is forming. Which is very rare. I've never seen this before. I'm sorry it's not the answer you want."

"It isn't, but it's reality, I suppose."

"Allōs, you needn't worry. You have a chance of salvation, but it will be an arduous journey for you to achieve. You have to want this and you cannot give in to the Xorraths. There is one catch."

"Oh?"

"To find salvation I'll have to send you to Earth." I felt Allōs's mood completely change. He looked down into his tea and was quiet for a moment and then he spoke.

"I should tell the Omegas that I have to leave." He tapped his ring and watched it blink until a ghostly image of Gabriel answered.

"Al, you're awake! That's amazing! We'll be there soon. Gabriel's image disappeared into the ring and a blinding light flashed at Mother's door.

There was a soft knock at the door and Mother waved them in. They all came inside and gathered around.

"Allōs!" Noah bolted to him and hugged Allōs as hard as he could.

"I missed you, Noah."

"How was it?"

"My coma?"

"What do you think, mate?"

"It was strange. I met my inner demon."

"That's odd. Not many angels have those," Gabriel said, as he twirled his hair.

"Why are you nervous, Gabe?"

"I just am. I don't want to lose you, Al."

"Stop. You're going to make me cry." Gabriel got up and hugged the hell out of Gabriel.

"I love you, Gabe, and sorry for what happened in the war room."

"You're good, Al, I promise." Jophiel got up and buried Allōs in her arms. "I missed you, Allōs. Everything hasn't been the same while you were gone. But tell us about your journey. I'm really curious about what you experienced," she said.

"Alright, as long as all of you update me about the war."

"Deal."

Al sat down at the couch as everyone huddled around him.

"My time trapped in myself was strange. I met a Xorrath. His name was Ovelth."

"Oh shit, you met a Xorrath!"

"Language, Gabe."

"Sorry, Mother. What was it like, Allōs?"

"Scary. He says he wants to kill me, plain and simple. It's beyond scary knowing that something inside you wants you dead."

"That sounds awful, Al."

"It is, Chamuel. Oh, I have some really bad news for all of you." Everyone looked at Allōs and held their breath. "I have to go to Earth to sort this nightmare out."

"Why?" They all asked in unison.

"I don't know yet. Mother and I still have to talk about that another time. Just do me a favor, Gabriel. Please don't replace me."

Gabriel smiled at his comment and assured him that he wouldn't. "Everyone," Mother said, "you might want to say your goodbyes, then Luke, Allōs, and I need to discuss a few things."

The Omegas reluctantly said their goodbyes, and before everyone was about to leave, we turned to Allōs and deeply bowed.

"It's been an honor serving with you, Allōs the Blue," we all said together.

"Likewise, my friends." He responded and bowed in return. Mother, Allōs, and I watched everyone fly back to the northern front.

Mother said, "Come, we have much to discuss."

"Al, are you really leaving us?"

"I think so, unless there's another way," he said, as he gestured to Mother.

"Allōs, I really wish there was another way," Mother said. "I really hate sending you to Earth. And I hate separating you and Luke even more. However, I have my reasons for sending you there. Allōs, when you get to Earth, find a man by the name of Jamie O'Meara. He will help you cope. Anyway, I'll give you two some privacy," Mother said as she walked off into another room.

"Al, don't worry about me, babe. Also, don't fall too hard for Jamie."

"I won't, Luke. You are mine after all."

I smiled and said, "Mother has a great plan in place for you. As long as I know you're safe then I'll be fine. Just remember, I'll be here when you get back." I smiled again, but behind my smile was absolute sadness. I did my best to try to hide it like I always do. I held Allōs's hand as we sat there in varying states of shock.

"I don't doubt Mother's plan, but this is all just happening so fast. What have I left undone to deserve this? Everything feels different to me. I can't put my finger on it. It just feels off. I don't want to leave you, Luke. Will I see you again?"

"I don't know, babe." I shrugged. Allōs looked at me, and judging by his look he knew that I was about to cry. "I'm going to miss you, babe." Allōs hugged me and I felt his shirt begin to dampen. "I don't want to lose you, especially when I don't know when I'll see you again."

"Luke, stay strong. Do me a favor?" I looked up at him.

"Sure, what?"

"Get close with Noah. He'll help you through this."

"I can't do that to you."

"You think I feel comfortable starting this journey with Jamie?"

"Fair point, Allōs. I'll get close to Noah, but only for you."

I tightened my grip on him. I knew I'd have to let go soon, but I didn't want to. Allōs could sense this and pulled me into a passionate kiss that I knew meant he was saying the final goodbye. When my eyes met his again, I saw his green eyes stare back at me and I knew it was time.

"I love you always, Allōs."

"I love you too, Luke." With aching hearts Allōs and I walked to the door. I spread my wings and soared off into the distance.

Chapter 6

Mother walked into the room and sat next to me.

"I wouldn't call my plan great, but it *is* a plan."

"It can't get any worse at this point. By the way, did you give me a tattoo?"

"I have. I hope you like it."

"I do Mother. It's very you."

Mother smiled. "Allōs, as you've come to realize, you will be starting this journey with no powers."

"Unfortunately so. Will I ever get them back?"

"Yes, as I said before, talk to my sister. We'll go into more details when you arrive on Earth. As I said earlier, when you get to the earthly plane, you're going to meet a man by the name of Jamie O'Meara. He will help you and he will be a friend when you need one most. So keep him close, Allōs."

"There's so many people on Earth. How am I supposed to know what he looks like?"

"You'll know him when you see him. Unfortunately, we don't have any more time that I can give you. Come fly with me."

I nodded and spread my wings. We soared up to the top of her mountain to perch ourselves so that we could gaze at Heaven for this last time. Heaven was a mess. Large scorch marks tarnished the landscape. Seeing my home like this broke my heart.

"I'm going to miss this place." I looked at the sleek modern landscape, or what was left of it, and took it in.

Mother swiped her arm dismissively, palm outward, summoning a large swirling portal at the base of her mountain.

"This is it, my son – the start of your journey and where we must part ways. Good luck, and you needn't fear, I will be there to guide you. Remember your armor can serve you well in time of need. I'll be there in a few days after you land in Ireland." She smiled wryly as she gathered me into a touchingly gentle and warm embrace.

"So I meet Jamie and everything will fall into place?"

"Yes, in due time." She pulled back to tap my chest and my armor began enveloping me. She raised her hand and I started levitating, and she threw me off the mountain. I spread my wings and started soaring through the sky with the fury of God at my heels.

My mind whirled as I was thrown into Mother's portal and enveloped in a realm of darkness scattered with stars. A sentence from a book I'd once read popped into my mind: 'Space is known for its vast emptiness with some of it occupied by varying planets and stars, the latter of which give off a glow that can be seen across the cosmos even after that star has died.' *So this is space.* I looked around, trying to take in as much of it up close as I could while I hurtled toward Earth at a breakneck pace. I broke through the atmosphere, bursting into flames and rocketing to Earth. I looked around and saw a vast ocean and a small dot of an island, which grew bigger and bigger till I came crashing into the south-eastern shoreline of Ireland. It was too dark to tell where I was, but I knew that I had crashed into a small lagoon with a large stone wall in front of me, causing the ground to shake.

"Fuck, that hurt!" I tried to stand up but I fell to the ground. I tapped my chest and my armor receded into my skin, as my ring flashed blue. *I always forget that I have this ring. I remember when I was given it. From that point on, I knew I was an archangel. I was so excited when Gabriel gave me this.* I tried taking off my ring but it didn't budge. It was still attached to my skin. *So it's not as hopeless as I thought.*

A light surrounded me; I looked down and saw I was no longer dressed in what I normally wear. Instead, I was costumed in something more primitive, more plain, a tee shirt, jeans, and boots. "Ugh, what the hell are these clothes? Earth, you have got to get a fashion sense." I held out my hand to summon my glaive, but nothing happened. "That's right, no powers, damn it!" I found a piece of driftwood lying next to me. I picked it up and tried to use that for support and it snapped. I lay there face first in the sand in total defeat.

I spread my wings and started to gently float over the ground. I was shocked to realize that I was able to fly here. Though, it doesn't take any magic to fly, which is nice. As I flapped my wings, the sand began to stir; I hovered about the beach for a few minutes.

What time is it? I looked around and all I saw was darkness. I flew up to the road and looked into the distance and saw the lights of a town up ahead. I slowly placed myself on the ground and retracted my wings. I then realized something: I was alone for the first time in a long time. With my reality threatening to break me, I put one foot in front of the other, trying to not fall on my face. I made my way methodically toward the town.

The town drew nearer as my hearts grew heavier. I reached for my pocket and realized that my cigarettes had vanished with my other clothes. *Fuck this day, I just need* something. With a sigh

75

I passed the outskirts of the town and ended up stumbling upon a bar that was tucked into a corner that suited my needs just fine. *A drink is better than nothing.*

Soft lights eased my transition from the darkness of night. I opened the door and was greeted by an empty atmosphere. An extensive collection of alcohol lined the shelves behind the bar. I slouched down into one of many vacant stools, choosing one right next to the entrance. I was greeted by a tall, pale, soft-featured man with flowing black hair that draped down his back.

"Welcome to O'Meara's," he said. "My name is Jamie. What can I get you?"

"Something strong."

"Can do!" He pulled down a bottle of whiskey and poured me a glass on the rocks. I looked up to thank him. He was wearing a long-sleeved, black tee shirt and blue jeans. *He's cute. I wouldn't mind if he was the guy I'm supposed to look for. I wonder what his name is.* What he said earlier clicked in my head: Jamie O'Meara. *That was easy enough.* I heard a soft clink as Jamie placed my drink in front of me.

"Thank you."

"You look awful, man. It looks like you crashed head first into Dunmore beach."

I couldn't help but laugh at how shockingly accurate his statement was. I looked down and saw I was covered in sand.

"It definitely felt like it. Ever have one of those days?"

"Loads of times, but I usually grab a pint with the mates and forget about my troubles."

"You wouldn't happen to have a cigarette on you?"

"I don't smoke personally, though you can get a pack of fags up the road."

76

I folded my arms and rested my head on the bar and started to drift into space. The sound of shifting glasses and footsteps filled my head.

"So, where are you visiting from?"

I froze; I hadn't considered that I would have to come up with a backstory that was plausible while I was here. *Things just got a whole lot more complicated.*

"Just…from out of town."

"Okay, I'll be more specific. You sound American, so which part of America are you from, if you don't mind me asking?"

The only thing I could blurt was the only knowledge of America that the archives had given me.

"I'm from California."

"What's it like there?"

I had no clue how to proceed since the archives had only given me a very limited description of what Earth was like, let alone a specific country.

"Um, just like any standard metropolitan city. I know that's not really the answer you were looking for, but it's an apt description."

"I guess I'll just have to believe you." He winked at me. "So, what's your name?"

"My friends call me Al." I continued to sip on my whiskey.

"Is it short for Alfred?" he asked with glee.

"Umm…maybe. Why?"

"I just really like Alfred Pennyworth."

"Who?"

"He's just the *best* butler in the world because he works for the one and only Batman."

"Ohh."

"Anyway, it is my pleasure to formally welcome you to Ireland, Al. What brings you here?"

I glanced at my sapphire ring and I could feel the sadness in me pooling in my eyes before I could stop it.

"I've moved here to sort something out."

"Interesting. Are all Americans as dark and mysterious as you, or is it just a you thing?"

"It's just a me thing really. Though, I'm not usually this depressed."

"Must've been quite the journey." He started putting glasses away, seeming in the process of closing for the night. "Seems like it would be lonely though, leaving a familiar place behind."

"It was tough, but it was needed for my own state of mind." I shifted as if to get up. "You seem to be closing, so I can get out of your hair if you need."

"Don't even think about it. I was enjoying the conversation and even more so the company." He smiled at me.

I smiled back in response and let my eyes wander over his extensive alcohol collection behind the bar. He had quite the variety, all of which I knew, except for name brands. Earth felt kind of strange and disjointed from what I was used to, making me crave the simplicity and familiarity that only home can offer.

"You alright, Al?"

My eyes regained their focus on Jamie's perturbed face.

"Yeah...I'm just," I sighed in defeat, "sad, I guess."

"You know what me mam always said to me when I was sad?"

I shook my head.

"She would say, 'Jamie, look at everything you have, and then look at what other people have. Some are much worse off than you.'"

"She's not wrong," I whispered to myself somberly, smiling wryly before lacing my words with some venom. "Though it's never really healthy to compare your own life to that of others." I was bitterly trying to keep my composure and not cry with rage; which, thankfully, Jamie was picking up on and he didn't take my outburst to heart.

"I served and protected my family, my home, and my fellow man just as I was sworn to do without fail. And because of something out of my control, I was cast out to find my salvation." I let out a defeated sigh.

"I've found that living your life according to other people's expectations, no matter how hard you try, always ends up in disappointment."

"He speaks a truth for someone so primitive, and he seems rather enlightened as well," Ovelth whispered.

I slammed back my drink. I ignored Ovelth as best I could, but I wasn't able to shake the thought that they both might have a point. *Maybe they're right. I've placed my faith in something that didn't offer as much in return and has abandoned me in my time of need.* My thoughts scattered as they were interrupted by Jamie's faint Irish accent and his voice drifted into my mind.

"Out of all that's happened, surely there must be something good that could come out of it?"

"Can't say for sure about anything at the moment." I gave him a fake smile. "Sorry, I'm just not in a good place right now to think about it, and as far as I can tell you're the only silver lining that comes to mind."

"I'm not all that special, Al. Another round?"

"Sure! Why not?"

Jamie happily smiled as he poured me another drink.

"What's got you so happy?"

"Oh nothing. I don't get people as cute as you coming here all that often. Plus you can hold a conversation."

"That was a conversation? That felt more like a therapy session."

"I didn't mind. I find it interesting. It gives me a chance to look into a person's mind." Jamie walked to the doors and flipped the open sign to closed. "Hey, Al, I have nothing to do tomorrow. Care to slam some pints?"

"I mean...I'm not going to pass up the opportunity to drink with a nice stranger such as yourself."

"Fuck, yeah!"

"Why are you so nice to me Jamie?"

"Well, you don't seem like a serial killer to me plus I find you interesting."

"I mean I could be a serial killer and you just don't know it."

"True, but wouldn't you have killed me by now?"

"You have a point." I finished my drink as Jamie handed me a pint of black beer.

"What's this?"

"It's Guinness."

"What?"

"I've never met anyone who doesn't know what Guinness is. I guess there's a first for everything."

"Oh there's always a first for everything, Jamie."

"You dirty fucker."

I stuck out my tongue playfully at Jamie. I took a sip of the Guinness and it was more bitter than I expected. I expected it to be creamy and chocolatey, but I liked the bitterness.

"Thanks for the beer!"

"You like it?"

"Hell, yeah."

"So, Al, tell me a bit about yourself?"

"My name is Allōs the Blue, I'm an arch—" I stopped dead in

80

my tracks, realizing that humans wouldn't believe me if I dropped the fact that I'm an archangel.

"An arch what? Archangel?"

I didn't know what to do. He did say it, but I knew I couldn't tell him the truth. I would definitely sound like a serial killer then. *What do I say?* I could lie my way out of this, but I couldn't. *Fuck! I'm trapped!*

"Allōs, you okay? You went quiet on me."

"What?" I shook my head. "Yeah I'm fine. I just don't know how to articulate myself."

"Then forget about it. If you don't want to talk about it, then don't."

"I'm fine with talking about it. I just can't give too much information away."

"Oh shit! Are you part of a secret military unit or something?"

"Yes…let's go with that." I took another sip of my beer and noticed that it got more bitter as it sat out.

"Is it supposed to be more bitter as it sits out?"

"I think so. I don't drink it much."

"Ah, I like it though. But to answer your question, I am military. Special forces, I suppose."

"Most impressive, my friend."

I finished off my beer. "Got any more?"

"What, beer?"

"Could I go back to the whiskey?"

"Yeah sure!" Jamie grabbed a small glass and joined me at the bar and poured himself a drink.

"So tell me about you."

"Well, my name is Jamie O'Meara. I'm twenty-four. I'm a full-time barman, huge nerd, nothing special really," he said, as he sipped his drink.

"I'm pretty sure you're special in more ways than you think."

"Perhaps."

"Jamie, where am I?"

"Like here in Ireland?"

"Yeah."

"We're in Dunmore East in County Waterford."

"Am I supposed to know what that means?"

Jamie pinched the bridge of his nose.

"For fuck sakes," he whispered under his breath. "Don't worry, you're not the only one who has no clue where we are. How long are you here for?"

"Probably a few years. I could use a guide to show me around."

"You got a deal. I'd love to show you around. Sounds fun."

"You sound fun."

"So I've been told, Al." Jamie winked as he took another sip. "Where are you staying?"

"I haven't figured that out yet."

"There's a few Airbnbs around here, so I doubt you'll have any trouble finding a place. If you really need a place, I can let you crash here for a night or so."

"I might take you up on that offer."

"It's a deal, cheers."

We clinked our glasses and continued chatting for a few hours as Jamie got progressively more drunk.

"I need to head to bed!" Jamie said as he hobbled off to bed.

"Night, Jamie."

"Oh! I'm sorry I don't have a bed for you, but there is a couch and there are blankets in the other room."

"Thanks, man. I'll see you in the morning."

"For sure. Night, Allōs." Jamie went to bed and shut the door behind him.

82

"Night, Jamie." I said as I continued drinking. I didn't finish off the bottle; I would feel bad if I did. I placed my forehead on the bar and sighed.

Ugh! This day could have been worse I suppose and fuck, Jamie is cute. Maybe Mother is onto something – he's really kind and sweet, and funny. Ugh, I need a walk.

I cleaned the glasses and put the liquor away and headed outside. The town was small and cozy. It reminded me of Mother in a way. A slight chill brushed past me along with a few other people wandering the streets drunkenly. Light from the full moon pulled my gaze upward, causing me to wonder: *Is that the same moon that we see in Heaven? Doubtful; Heaven and Earth have been separated for so long that I doubt this world even knows where it came from.* I looked around, trying to get my bearings so as to make my way out of town. I decided to head north and hopefully hit the edge, until a soft voice stopped me in my tracks.

"Hello, Allōs. I'm glad to see you made it here unharmed."

"You could have told me to jump, you know, Mother."

"I know, but I miss using my power."

"Uh huh, you didn't have to throw me that hard."

Mother gave me a cheeky smile. "Don't deny a goddess her pleasures."

"Throwing your child off of a mountain is a pleasure?"

"Well, when you put it like that, Allōs, you make me sound like a monster."

I smiled. "What are you doing here, Mother?"

"Just came to check up on you. What do you think of Jamie?"

"He's so sweet, and cute. Don't tell Luke I said that."

"My lips are sealed."

"Speaking of which, how is he?"

"He's handling it better than I thought he would."

"He's stronger than everyone gives him credit for Mother. He's been through hell and back with me and he still stands by my side."

Let's take a walk, Allōs." She sedately strolled next to me. "I know you dislike being here. Just promise me something." She turned her eyes encouragingly toward me. "Don't lose your faith."

"Ha! What has faith done for you?!" Ovelth scoffed.

I shook my head.

Mother noticed, and said, "What is Ovelth saying now?"

"Oh nothing. He's just making a case as to why faith is meaningless. You know, the usual."

"Ah, like I said before, please don't lose faith."

"I'm simply confused as to how and why this has happened to me. I've done everything right up until this point. I served God as well as Heaven practically since I was born. Because of one mess-up in the cosmic order, I lose everything. I don't even know why I'm really here, Mother. All I want to know is, why me? The voice in my head is dismantling everything, making me doubt you and all I know." I stared down at my hands. "Am I a demon now? What's going to happen to me?"

"Allōs, you're spiraling. You're still the Archangel Allōs the Blue. You haven't turned yet – that's all that matters. I know you don't believe this, but I don't know what's ahead. More accurately, what's to come is unclear to me. I know you have anger in your soul, but it wasn't enough to breed a demon on its own. So what happened?"

"There was Lucifer."

"Oh yeah, that's true. But as of now, no, you're not a demon. And you have the power to keep it that way."

"But I don't have my powers to keep Ovelth at bay."

"I know it's frustrating. Speak with my sister. She can help you."

"Who is your sister?"

"Her name is Danú. Good night, Allōs, and I'll see you soon. Remember this, I love you. Keep Jamie close to you. He'll be one of your closest allies. Rest easy," Mother said. She cupped the side of my face and disappeared into the wind without a trace.

Chapter 7

I flew to the beach, landed, and started wandering aimlessly. I felt myself being beckoned to sleep. I propped myself against a rock and reluctantly answered the call of sleep. When I opened my eyes, Ovelth stood among the darkness waiting for me, gently floating while his eyes were the only source of light.

"What now?"

"I say only this – perhaps you have something more inside you than you would have thought. Things more malicious and indifferent than you would like them to be, child."

"Look, if you're going to be here for a while, you might as well tell me what the hell you're saying."

"Look inside yourself and you will find the answer."

"I am inside myself! So what are you hinting at, Ovelth?!"

Ovelth let out a deep chuckle as he started to circle around me. "I am here merely to remind you of who you truly are," he said, as he wrapped his ghostly body around me.

I braved the pain as he dug his claws into my shoulder...

"Now wake, child."

I woke up and was greeted by Mother.

"I thought you left for the night."

"In a moment, love. I'm just concerned that you're sleeping more than you should. Like I said before, the dream realm is

86

a cursed place, and I'm curious what Ovelth wants." Mother helped me up to my feet. I brushed myself off.

"Ovelth is getting rather annoying."

"Oh, is he now? Did he say anything worth mentioning?"

"He said that he was here to remind me of who I truly am. Why are angels wary of the earthly plane?"

"You're changing the subject, Allōs, but to answer your question, this plane is ravaged by war, hatred, and sin. Sin on this plane attaches itself to whomever the sinner is — unlike in Heaven. But I want to hear more about Ovelth."

"In a moment, but sin really works like that?"

"Yes, Allōs. Humans are much more prone to it due to the inherent nature of both them and this plane. I've never seen such blind hypocrisy about God until I ventured to this plane."

I cocked my head. "What do you mean?"

"Humans are a tricky bunch, especially when it comes to religion. Some use God to persecute others simply because they don't worship the same. Which to me makes no sense because they all worship the same god at the end of the day. Ugh, if there's one absolute thing I hate about humans it is that they are so petty. Sometimes the pettiness of humans astounds me."

"That doesn't surprise me in the slightest. What role does Lucifer play here?"

"Well, he wanders Earth enticing people to sin so he can trap them into an eternity of servitude and damnation."

"So he recruits people into his army, essentially?"

"Yes. But get this, some people voluntarily join his army."

"Huh, strange. But Ovelth didn't say anything interesting in my opinion. He's just toying with me at this point. It's not like we're having heart-to-heart conversations about our likes and dislikes."

Mother smiled at me and the conversation stuttered into silence. She had a look of fear in her eyes.

"What's wrong, Mother?"

"Nothing. I'm just losing another child to the darkness, and I will not let that happen." Mother handed me a pack of cigarettes. "I got these from your apartment. I thought you'd want to have something from home with you."

"Thanks." I rolled my eyes and continued staring at the water. "What the hell am I supposed to light these with?"

"A candle, match, lighter – flint and steel if you're desperate enough. You'll figure it out. I have all the confidence in you, Allōs."

I stood there in confusion. "Okay then. Will I see you soon?"

"Of course you will. You should get some rest," Mother said, as she walked into the ocean and disappeared with the tides.

I lay down in the sand and listened to the tide slap against the shore. Listening to the waves lulled me into a comfortable place and I let my mind wander till morning. The following morning, my train of thought was interrupted by a boot in my side.

"Oi! Boyo, get up! Come on, let's go, you drunk," someone said as they nudged me with their boot. I heard a familiar voice, but I couldn't place it.

With a groan I rolled over toward them. "What is it now?" I faded back into reality and was surprised to see Jamie. "Jamie?"

"Al?" Jamie cocked his head in confusion. "What the hell are you doing out here?"

I got up from the ground and brushed myself off.

"I was enjoying the late-night tide till you interrupted me."

"You're sleeping outside? You could have slept at the pub." Jamie gave me a look of concern.

"I wasn't sleeping. I was staring at the ocean all night. What are you doing here anyway?"

"Taking a morning stroll. I was not expecting to see you here. Oh, and thanks for cleaning the bar. You really didn't have to."

"I know, but it was the right thing to do. I didn't want you to bother with dishes when you woke up."

"You're sweet. Here, follow me."

Jamie led me to a café down the road. He grabbed two menus and we sat down.

"So, Al, tell me about yourself."

"What do you want to know?"

"The basics, I suppose. Where you come from, what's your family like, stuff like that."

"Well, as I said, I'm from Cali. I didn't tell you about my family?"

"No, you only mentioned the fact that you are special ops military and then vented about how much your life sucked."

"You make me sound like such a little bitch."

"It's a gift." Jamie gave me a cheeky smile.

I leaned back in my chair. "Well, my family is a melting pot of people. There's Gabriel, Michael, Raphael, Jophiel, Azrael, Chamuel, Ariel, Noah, and Luke."

"Strange names, very…biblical. What are they like?"

Damn, he's right. Mother, who did you set me up with? A mind reader?

"Do you really want to dive down this rabbit hole?"

"I do."

"Well, Gabriel the Gold is very brotherly, loving, kind, boisterous at times, and a good teacher. Michael the Scarlet is more or less the father of the group. He keeps us together, plus

89

he's the best damned healer I've met. Raphael the Amethyst is the most militaristic of us all. He's very level-headed, but at times he would rather speak with his fists. Jophiel the Auburn is very loving, and we call her the sister of the group. Azrael the Royal is a complete mystery to me. Believe it or not, though, he is very sweet. Chamuel the Pewter is kind of a dick to be honest with you, mostly because he's arrogant as all hell. But, once you push through that barrier, he's actually a really nice guy. I know he gives that off because he doesn't want us to know that he's a big teddy bear. Ariel the Onyx is another sister of the group and she's stronger than we give her credit for."

"Why's that?"

"Mostly because she's usually very bubbly and lighthearted but recent events threw us into a dark spell."

"What happened?"

"Our home was attacked and we all felt a massive impending war at our doorstep." I fell silent, and gave a hollow stare at the table. I felt myself swell with sadness and tried to hold back the tears. Jamie caught on to my emotion.

"Allōs?"

"Yeah?"

"You don't have to talk about it. I'm sorry for bringing that up. I didn't want to make you upset."

"You're good."

"No, I'm really sorry for upsetting you, Al."

"Jamie, it's fine, I promise."

We were interrupted by a sharp voice carrying across the café. "Oi, Jamie, it's about time I saw your face around here! Where have you been?"

"Oh the usual – getting drunk, shifting some lads, and having the craic."

"And you didn't call me?"

"I would have, but it was boys only."

"Ah, you cheeky fucker. Who's this, one of the boys?"

I couldn't help but blush.

"You guessed it!" I said. "This man is a wonder! He made a man out of me! It was amazing." I winked at Jamie. He turned beet-red and looked like he was ready to kick me under the table.

"I like this one, Jamie. Keep him and don't fuck it up."

"I'll try not to, Morgan. What have you been up to?"

"Making music, actually. I'm almost done with my demo."

Jamie raised his eyebrows. "Oh, it's music now? Congratulations."

"What's that supposed to mean?"

"Well you do have a habit of picking up crafts and calling them your passions in life."

"It is though."

"You sure it's not just a phase?"

"It's not a phase! God, you're such a dick."

"You know you love me, Morgan."

Morgan rolled her eyes at him. "What can I get you?"

"I'll take my usual and one for him as well."

"What can I get you to drink, love?"

"I'll have a coffee."

"I'll get you a pot so you can split it."

"You're too kind." I looked around the café and thought that it was quite small, but it was nice actually. We were the only three in the café. It was cozy and brightly lit, the polar opposite of Jamie's bar. His bar used heavy woods, warm lighting, and had few windows; the café used lighter woods, natural lighting, and had many windows.

I turned to Jamie again. "So, how did you meet Morgan?"

91

"We go way back. We were friends through primary school and all through college. But I distinctly remember going into clubs with her when we were sixteen, I think it was. God, that was an interesting phase for me."

"Fuck off, Jamie! It wasn't a phase! You were just as willing to get into trouble as I was. Don't act all high and mighty."

"I will be the highest and the mightiest, damn it!"

I rolled my eyes. "What did you study in college?"

"Psychology. However, my plans fell through so I learned to pull pints."

"Where did you go to college?"

"Dublin." Morgan came back with a pot of coffee and two cups for us.

"Thank you."

Morgan nodded.

I looked up at Jamie and noticed that he was studying me from head to toe, trying to figure me out. I took a moment to look him over and found myself thinking I wouldn't normally go for guys like him, but there was something about him that was alluring. Was it the hair? Or was it the fact that he was so damn nice. I didn't know. Either way, he was cute. I did feel slightly bad for thinking that, because I still love Luke. But I guess what he doesn't know won't hurt him.

"So, Jamie, tell me, how did you get your bar?"

"Well, my parents gave me a sum of money and told me to find a place to live and I bought a bar instead, because I hate flats. I'd rather own a place than rent one. You know what I mean?"

"I do. Why a bar though?"

Jamie took a sip of coffee. "Well, as I said before, I hate flats, so I had a wing added to the pub so I can live there. As for why a pub specifically, I've always liked serving people. I know it sounds strange, but I do. Plus my parents told me that I needed to get a job when my plans fell through. So I killed two birds with one stone by buying the pub."

"Very crafty."

"Thanks, Al."

A few moments later, Morgan arrived with our food, which was a full Irish breakfast.

"Thank you," Jamie and I said in unison.

This food was very different to what I was used to eating. I took a bite.

"Huh."

"What's up?"

"It's better than I thought."

"I'm glad you like it. This is one of my favorite places. So why Ireland?"

"What?"

"What made you come to Ireland, Al?"

You're just full of questions aren't you? I had no clue what to say to Jamie. I couldn't just say that I came to Ireland because of him. I had to come up with something.

"It's as far away from the Omegas as I can think of."

"What's that?"

"The Omegas? They are my family."

"Why are you trying to go away from your family?"

"Because they kicked me out because I have to face my inner demon. Which I honestly understand. But I wish it had played out differently." I took a few bites of my food and sipped my coffee.

Jamie cocked his head in confusion. "Is the military always that harsh?"

"Just the Omegas. They are the most elite group of trained

professionals I have ever met and had the honor of working with. Enough about me, tell me about you, Jamie."

"Before we get into me, why are the Omegas color-coded?"

"Honestly, I wouldn't know, Jamie. But from what I've heard, our colors reflect parts of our personality traits. But again, that's only what I've heard."

Jamie looked down and noticed my ring. "Does it have to do with your ring?"

"More than likely. I never asked Gabriel about that. Anyway, I want to know about you. You've taken my interest. Plus I might as well get to know my guide to Ireland."

"Yeah, that would help if we got to know each other, but in all honesty there isn't much to know," he said, as he rubbed the back of his neck.

"Jamie, in my lifetime, I have met thousands of people with a thousand different stories. There's always something to know about someone."

"Fair enough. Okay, I'll start with this – I'm the oldest of three brothers. I know it's way too early to get this deep with you but you opened yourself to me, and there's something about you, Al, that I trust. I don't know...I just feel like a fuck-up, to be honest with you. My younger brother, Scott, is planning on pursuing a doctorate at university and my youngest brother, Luke, is showing interest in pursuing law. And then there's me, a lowly barman. I just feel like I failed my parents, honestly. Also, I feel like I'm the black sheep of the family."

"Why's that?"

"I hit a low point in my life after my plans fell through. So I sought solace at the bottom of a glass and a few other things."

"Like what, if I may ask?"

"Drugs. Though had to stop because at my absolute lowest

94

point, they almost killed me. To the point where I didn't think I was coming back. So to combat that, I turned to tattoos and piercings for comfort. Let's just say that my family didn't like my choices when it came to my body modifications."

"What did you do to yourself?"

"I have one piercing and two tattoos now. I used to have a lot more piercings, but I took them out."

"What piercings do you have left?"

"Just my eyebrow."

"Wait really? I must have missed that. God, I'm slipping."

"Nah, I like to keep them somewhat hidden." Jamie pulled up his sleeve, exposing his right forearm. It was littered with angels and demons fighting one another; it was beautifully done. He pulled back the sleeve to his left arm and it was a beautiful geometric pattern. I looked up and noticed that his left eyebrow was pierced. How did that slip past me?

"What about you?" Jamie asked.

"I have a brand and one tattoo of a constellation on the right side of my chest."

"Like a cattle brand? They branded you?! That's fucked up, Al."

"It's not that bad."

"With all due respect, I'd beg to differ. You're a human, not cattle! No military should ever do that to their soldiers."

"If it makes you feel any better, it wasn't the Omegas who branded me. It was something else."

"What was it?"

"Just some crazy person that I was fighting. Anyway, how's the bar doing?"

"The pub is doing great. It's busy every night and there's a constant flow of money."

"So why do you feel the way you do?"

"Probably because I'm not a doctor or a lawyer."

"I think you're better off than your brothers, in my opinion. You're making money, and you seem happy enough."

"Maybe you're right, Al. Perhaps I'm too hard on myself."

A few hours passed as Jamie and I continued chatting and eating.

"Jamie, thank you for the meal. It means a lot to me. By the way, I need to ask you a favor."

"What's your favor?"

"Could I possibly crash at the pub for another night? I have nowhere to go. I can pay you back."

"Yeah sure. I don't see why not."

"Holy shit, really!? Thank you."

"No problem, Al. Also, if you need money, I can give you a job here if you want."

"Yes, that would be great."

"Do you have any experience being a barman?"

"No, but I'm a quick learner."

"Yeah, that's fine. I'm sure you'll do great." Jamie flagged down Morgan and paid the tab. "Al, what would you like to do now?"

"So, what is Dunmore like?"

"It's a fishing village, so it's a quiet place for the most part, that's really it. Everyone knows each other. You know, it's your typical village."

"That small?"

"Oh yeah, Ireland is a tiny country compared to America."

"Isn't there a coast near here?"

"Yeah, Dunmore beach. Want to go?"

"That sounds wonderful."

Chapter 8

As we were walking along the beach, I heard a faint but distinct voice whispering in my ear. It was the voice of a woman with a deep and harmonious voice. It wasn't Mother; it was someone else, someone I had never heard before.

"Fallen one, why are you here?"

I looked around to see if there was someone near me, and there was only Jamie. I thought nothing of it. I then heard the voice once more, but this time louder and more aggressive.

"You shouldn't be here, young one! Away with you, demon," the voice shouted.

"Shut up!" I whispered violently to myself, but Jamie heard and turned to me.

"Are you alright?"

"Absolutely peachy." My sarcastic tone came out a bit too harshly and Jamie narrowed his eyes at me. "Just intrusive thoughts, nothing more. Hey, Jamie, I hate to do this, but I'm going to smoke a cigarette. I'll be right back."

"Hey, take your time, man."

I smiled as I broke away and pulled out the pack of cigarettes that Mother had given me. I felt the presence of magic and it was strong here, very strong; however, it felt different. I couldn't place it though. I felt a pull to go to the water. I mindlessly went to the water and extended my hand and when I drew closer, I felt a surge of energy swelling in my fingertips. And upon touching the water a violent shock went rippling through my body. My hand recoiled.

"What the hell?"

"I told you, young one, you are not welcome here." The female voice grew louder.

I ignored the voice and wandered the beach looking for a lighter. A nice gentleman was kind enough to let me use his. I then started heading back to Jamie.

"Why are you pestering me?" I asked the voice.

"You're encroaching on the beings of my creation."

"Do you care to run that by me again?"

"You're meddling in the affairs of my child."

"Now wait just a moment. You're Jamie's mother?"

"In a way, yes. I am the Mother of all Celts."

"Wait, what now?"

"I'm sorry, my child, but you were raised in ignorance of other deities. My name is Danú, Mother of all Celts and Earth goddess of this land."

"Mother's sister?"

"Indeed, child. What do people call you?"

"Allōs the Blue. I am a former archangel, Mother Danú."

"So, how did you get to Ireland?"

"I was sent here by your sister."

"Very interesting. We'll discuss this later. Jamie is returning. Meet me here later tonight."

"How much later?"

"Whenever you can."

Jamie made his way to me. "Feel better?"

I smiled a bit as Jamie asked the question. "I do actually. Sorry for running off like that."

"No, you're fine."

From that point, Jamie and I wandered about the beach and talked.

"Hey, Al, want something to drink? And maybe watch a movie?"

"Um, sure."

With that, Jamie and I went back to the bar and to his living quarters. At the right side of his bar we entered a room, no larger than a one-bedroom apartment, that was fully furnished, including a kitchen.

"Hey, you want to choose the movie while I get the drinks? The remote is on the coffee table. I'm already logged in to my account so pick anything you want."

"Uh, sure." I went up to the TV and scanned the movie selections. I then noticed that he had a large DVD rack. My curiosity got the best of me. *Let's see here we have: a lot of* Star Wars *movies,* Jurassic Park, Back to the Future, ET, *a lot of superhero movies, and a lot of Harry Potter movies. What is all of this? I've never heard of any of these.*

"Hmm, what's *Star Wars* about?"

"You've never seen *Star Wars*?"

"Oh hey," I said, as Jamie handed me a whiskey, "what's the bottle for?"

"So we can have a good night, man, duh."

I cocked my head in confusion as to what he was trying to imply.

"Ah, for fuck sakes we just met. Although, I haven't been with an American...yet."

I rolled my eyes and ruffled his hair. We sat at opposite ends of the couch while we binged the franchise. Out of the corner of my eye, I noticed him looking at me from time to time, but

I paid him no mind. As the night marched on, and as Jamie got progressively more intoxicated, he drunkenly got up and stumbled to the doorway.

"Are you heading off to bed?"

"Yeah, I am way too drunk for my own good. Good night, Al."

"Night, Jamie."

Hours passed. I hadn't realized how tired I was; I was beckoned to sleep once more. I paused the movie and finished my drink. I looked around and found the blanket Jamie had mentioned last night. I grabbed the blanket and wrapped it around me before going to bed. When I fell asleep, I found myself in a massive, empty cathedral, one that I had never seen before. I slowly walked down the aisle while running my fingers across the pews. My train of thought was interrupted by a subtle breeze blowing behind me while a deep cackle reverberated throughout the church. A black cloud of smoke started to form. From out of that smoke, a man about six feet tall stepped out, clad in a black suit. He had clean-cut hair and a slight beard. His eyes were blue, and judging by his chin, he was clearly very buff.

"Hello, Allōs," he said in a rich voice that whispered in my ear. I whipped my head around and saw him standing behind me. I didn't know who he was, but he had this commanding presence that was very intimidating.

"Uh, hi. May I help you?"

"That's a very good question, Allōs. Can you help me? Or perhaps I can help you." Then the man vanished in a cloud and reappeared in the back of the church, sprawled out in a pew.

"I don't need help. Thanks though."

"Oh, but you do. Angels like yourself need so much more guidance. Especially because of your situation."

100

I paused for a moment and quickly tried to think of who this man could possibly be. "How do you know who I am?"

"I know much more than you would think, Allōs. You're the great executioner, eighth archangel of the Omegas."

By impulse I lifted my hand, and he started floating in the air. I felt a surge of rage ripple throughout my body and my eyes stung as they had when I first turned. I started forming a fist and the man's body started to crush from the inside out.

"I have my powers back? Strange."

"Not really, Allōs," he said, as he broke from my hold and straightened out his suit. "Ah, there are those beautiful blue eyes I've heard so much about."

In the blink of an eye the man was right in front of me, holding me by the jaw and looking deep into my eyes. His aura was dark and menacing and it put me on edge. Simply looking at this figure spiked my anger. I remembered this feeling. It was the feeling I had gotten when I was branded. I wanted to push him away, but I couldn't move. I struggled as hard as I could, but still could not move. I felt my life force being drained out of me. I felt myself getting weaker. I had to work up much strength to ask, "Who are you?"

"I go by many names, Allōs, all of which are unholy," he said, as he threw me across the church.

I gasped for air as I slowly felt myself grow back to health. This man walked toward me, and as he smiled maniacally, he revealed accentuated fangs.

"A demon."

"Good, my boy. But which one am I? So many to choose from."

I got back up and lunged at him with all my force with fireballs in hand. I was stopped by a force field in front of this

101

demon and then repelled backward. As I lay on the church floor, it hit me.

"Lucifer."

"Very good, Allōs. Now show me that power of yours!"

I whipped my arm up and a large stone cross erupted from the ground and I lunged forward, grabbing Lucifer by the throat and slamming him on the cross. I then summoned seven glaives and plunged all of them into his chest. For a moment Lucifer's body went limp and his eyes started to close slowly as he was lulled into a death-like state.

I jumped back and started saying, "Go in the name of God the Father and Son and the—" Then I heard hysterical laughter emanating from his body. I looked up and saw him twitch.

As he whipped up his head and looked at me with palpable hatred in his eyes, Lucifer pulled each blade from his chest.

"You can't kill me, Allōs. It's not that simple. God thinks that he is the be all and end all, but I'm his other half that he doesn't want to talk about! I keep this world in balance! I am the leader of this world, Allōs, and you will bow to me!"

"I will never bow to you," I said sharply.

Lucifer swiped his hand downward, and I fell to my knees.

"Look at me! You're mine, boy, and there's nothing you can do about it."

"What do you want with me?"

"Well, you're already one of us no matter how you cut it. I'm here to watch you fall. I'll start with this."

Lucifer snapped his fingers and my brand started to glow and seared with pain. I felt my eyes glowing with hatred while I started speaking in an ancient tongue. My wings gently lifted me to my feet. He grabbed me by the throat and put his thumb on my forehead. My anger subsided and my body went limp.

He then dropped me and my body hit the floor.

"You'll wake up a much different man, Allōs. You'll thank me later. Now wake up." He snapped his fingers.

Chapter 9

I opened my eyes and got up from the couch. I groaned and poured myself a drink and rubbed my eyes. I looked at the clock; it read two in the morning.

"What the fuck happened?" I felt my chest and arm burning. "So it was real. Fascinating." I snapped my fingers and nothing happened but the spark. "So my powers didn't cross over, damn it!"

I stumbled to my feet and turned on the light and looked at my arm. I saw that it was covered in markings that looked like ink smudges at first glance. But upon closer inspection the smudges turned into distorted faces that looked as if they were in eternal pain and as if they wanted to rip themselves from my skin. I walked to the nearest mirror and took my shirt off. The demented figures carried up to my chest, surrounding my Omega crest. I studied the markings in depth; there was something oddly beautiful about them. The beauty of these markings quickly went away when I felt a wave of sadness that pulsed through my body. I tried to fight the urge to cry.

"No, don't cry, Allōs. You're not done yet. This isn't the end for you! Pull yourself together! You're the executioner, for God's sake! It's just a marking, that's all." I wiped the tears from my face and looked at myself in the mirror. I rested my forehead on the glass and just let my mind wander for a few moments. I looked up at myself again and dabbed my eyes with the heels of my hands. I took a deep breath and reassured myself that I wouldn't be a nervous wreck.

There was a soft knock nearby. I turned around and found Jamie standing in the doorway. I quickly covered my chest, trying to hide the brand.

"Hey, what are you doing up, Al?"

"Oh shit, did I wake you up?"

"No, I was already up. Couldn't sleep. I never sleep well when I'm drunk." His shocked face quickly switched to concern, probably because of my red-rimmed eyes.

"Are you alright? Do you need to talk, Al? Is that the brand you were talking about?"

I felt my seven hearts jump at me. "Yeah."

Jamie came closer and ran his fingers across my chest with saddened curiosity. *Can he not see the tattoos? Strange. Lucifer, what did you mark me with?* Jamie followed the design with his finger. "An Omega, interesting," Jamie said softly. "Oh, sorry for just touching you, my bad."

"You're good. It's just hard, Jamie, you know."

Jamie held me in his arms and reassured me that everything would be alright. "Hey, look at me."

I looked up at Jamie and he looked me dead in the eyes and said, "You're going to get through this, Al. Trust me. Can you do that for me?"

I couldn't help but think that Jamie was much more kind than I would have expected from a human. It's completely unexpected for me at least, though why would I think that Mother would ever lead me astray?

"No, I can't do that right now. Why are you so nice to me?"

Jamie led me into the main room and sat down on one of the stools. "It's the right thing to do, Al." He poured me a drink.

"You would make a very good Omega."

"I don't think I have the skill for such a thing but thank you. Seriously though, what did they do to you?"

"As I said before, they didn't do anything to me. It was this hooded figure that had me pinned to a wall and branded me. I didn't see who it was though." I sat soberly at the bar and then got up and said, "Danú! I need to see her! I hope I'm not too late!"

"Who?"

"Mother Danú."

"From Celtic mythology?"

"Exactly. Hey, I'll be back, okay?"

"Where are you going?"

"Dunmore beach!"

"Why?"

"To talk to her!"

I frantically threw on a shirt and put my shoes on and went outside and flew to Dunmore beach. When I landed, the water was quiet and calm. The moon's pale light reflected on the ocean. The water started to stir and then began to glow. From out of the depths of the sea a beautiful woman emerged from the waves. She was taller than I had expected. Her body was in perfect proportion to itself from her torso to her hips. She had the sharpest jawline I've ever seen on a woman, but on her it worked beautifully. She wore a loose, flowing gown with Celtic symbols embroidered all across it.

"Hello, Allōs," she said in her deep voice.

"Good evening, Mother Danú. I'm sorry I'm late."

"I was beginning to think you weren't coming. Also, what troubles you, child?"

"Nothing, Mother Danú."

"Your heart betrays you, child. It's chaotic and unbalanced."

"Just had a bad dream, that's all."

"Allōs, we're not going to get anywhere if you're not going to be honest with me."

"Alright, I had this dream, and I met Lucifer and he marked me, and I don't know why. He said he wants to watch me fall. When I woke up my left arm was covered in demented tattoos."

Danú said, "Strange markings. I know not who they belong to."

"They belong to Lucifer." She nodded in understanding and looked into my eyes while gently holding my face. "Your soul does have much anger within it. But I do see much good in you, however. You want your powers back, don't you?"

"You'd just give them to me?"

"Yes."

"Why?"

"Because I believe this is the only way that you can get them back."

"The only way?"

"Yes, the markings that you bear prevent you from accessing your powers. I can help unblock those pathways. Follow me, young one."

Danú led me to the sea. We gently walked atop the water and she held me by the hand and pushed away from us, rocketing us far into the moonlit horizon. She touched the water and it started to glow. She flicked her two fingers down and I immediately fell through the surface of the water and Danú grew smaller and smaller. My vision went darker and darker until everything was completely black.

"Young one, can you hear me?"

107

"Yes, my lady."

"Focus on the healing powers of the waters around you."

The water felt like nothing I've ever felt before. It was calming. I felt at peace with my mind, body, and spirit. I closed my eyes and meditated, focusing on the water around me. I focused on my point of power and I felt my body growing warmer as the water around me began to stir. I whipped my head up and opened my eyes. I could feel my eyes glowing; this time it was calm and peaceful, it was familiar, it was happy. I felt my body getting hotter and hotter, causing the water to violently boil! I rocketed my way toward the surface with all the force my body could muster. I erupted from the depths of the sea, causing water to explode everywhere with a gentle rainfall. I shook the residual water off my wings. I paused for a moment with skepticism, not knowing if I truly had my powers back or not. I snapped my fingers and a small blue flame hovered above my thumb. I then held out my hand and my glaive appeared in my palm. I summoned fifty more glaives, and they hovered in front of me silently. I swatted at the air and my weapons disappeared. I then held out my hand and a flame danced in my palm. I let the flame grow bigger and bigger; it started climbing over my arm till it enveloped me completely. I summoned as much fire as I could muster and moved my arms in such a way that the flames encased Danú and me in a massive ball of fire that moved perpetually around us. This ball lit up the night sky like a lighthouse. I let the light rage for a few moments before casting it into the sky and letting it explode and rain down a dazzling blue.

"For an archangel, you're very reckless."

I pulled out a cigarette and proceeded to light it. I closed my eyes, inhaled. "I realize that. There's probably going to be a press release or something. Ugh, what did I just do?"

"Created a problem for yourself." She chuckled. "Does Jamie know?"

"Know what?"

"Everything."

I stopped for a moment and then looked at her and said, "No. I've given him bits and pieces about my past that would make sense for a human to understand, but as for telling him I'm not human, no. Plus I've only known him for two days. It would be too soon."

"He's much more understanding than you think, Allōs. You should tell him."

"But how?"

"Just give him time."

I took another drag. Danú and I came to the shoreline and we heard a distant call.

"Al?"

I jumped back and without thinking I summoned a glaive and pointed it into the shadows with a flame at the ready on the other hand.

From out of the light, Jamie stepped forth. "Al..." Jamie stood there in shock. He looked at me, Danú, my glaive, and the fire I had in my hand. "I take it that this is Danú?"

"That is correct, Jamie."

"So magic is real, Danú?"

"Yes."

"God?"

"Yes," I answered.

"So I'm fucked?"

"Yes, but so am I if that makes you feel any better." I said.

"So what are you, Allōs?"

"An archangel."

109

"Focus, children," Danú chimed in. "Jamie, I know it must be hard to understand, but as I said to Allōs, you were raised in ignorance. However, it's not your doing. Just know this, stay close to Allōs. He will protect you from what will unfold in the near future. I sense a war brewing here on Earth. It will arrive just as quickly as it will end, catching humans in the crossfire."

"Mother Danú, the war is going to bleed out onto Earth?"

She said, "There was a war in Heaven?"

"It's known as the Second Demon War. It broke out three months ago."

"Allōs, tell me more of this impending war. Here, take a seat." Mother Danú gently lifted her hand and three blocks of stone rose from the beach, resembling a table and chairs. We gathered at the table. I snapped my fingers and a large plain decanter, three cups, and two candles appeared on the table. I poured Danú a drink then one for Jamie and myself. I took a sip and lit the candles.

"As I said before, the war broke out three months ago and the attack is being led by Mephistopheles."

"Strange. I wonder what he wants with Heaven."

"The Omegas and I believe that Mephisto is doing this to create chaos to garner the attention of Lucifer. But he's never been successful, and I doubt that he will be. But I can't shake the feeling that the Omegas failed at containing the Flock."

"Allōs, I understand that you're concerned, but I never said that the Omegas failed. Not to mention they have my sister fighting on their side."

"How do you know that?"

"If I know my sister, she's desperate to fight. She was the warrior out of the two of us. I don't doubt the capabilities of the Omegas, let alone the holy spirit."

"How did she become the holy spirit?"

110

"Loreley became the holy spirit when God found her thousands of years ago. He offered her a job essentially to care for all of the newborn angels and to carry out his will on Earth."

"Sister, you don't give me enough credit. I'm far more than just a mother and the will carrier of God."

We all whipped our heads round and looked at the darkness. Mother stepped out from the shadows.

"Hello, Mother. I was wondering when you were going to show up."

"Hello, Allōs, Jamie, Danú. I do apologize for crashing the party. I know it's rude of me."

"No, it's fine. I don't mind a surprise visit from my sister. It's nice to see you again. How are things?" Danú raised her hand up and another chair appeared.

Mother slumped down in her chair. "Challenging, but good. Which reminds me, Allōs, I have an update for you."

I gestured to Mother and took a sip of my drink. "How are the Omegas? How's Luke?"

"They're good. They reclaimed the northern mountain range and they're holding that position, so that's good. Luke is surviving. I've never seen him like this before. He's not as bubbly as he used to be and I fear it's only going to get worse. He really misses you. You should contact him."

"I'll be sure to do that."

"You should – he'd really appreciate that. There's no new threat on the horizon. Everything is stable."

"Not for long, Loreley. I foresee war plaguing the Earth in the near future."

"I sense it too, and I hate to admit that. I knew this war was going to get out of hand, but Mephistopheles is being much more aggressive than usual."

111

Danú rose from her chair and plucked at the air and a thin golden line materialized in front of us.

"You can access the eternal timeline?"

Danú smiled. "Yes, Allōs. But, everyone, this is my concern." Danú hovered her fingers over a point in the timeline where it spiked. "Right here." Danú touched the spike and images of total destruction enveloped the land: Ireland in ruin, fires everywhere, and these twisted bird creatures swarming over everything.

"What are those things?" Jamie asked timidly.

"I know not where they come from, or who commands them, but they will bring destruction to my home," Danú said.

"Sounds like the Flock made its way here," I said.

"Who commands them, Allōs?"

"Mephistopheles, Mother Danú."

"So what does this mean for Earth, Al?" Jamie asked.

"I wish I knew, Jamie. I have a feeling that the Omegas will be here soon. Then, from that point I wouldn't know."

"Fear not, Allōs, about what is to come. The Omegas will be triumphant but at cost. And there are some things I must stay quiet on," Danú interjected.

"Danú, will you be fighting with us?"

"Loreley, if I have to defend my home then that is what I shall do."

"Al, what do you need me to do?"

"I need you to stay alive, Jamie. I'll do my best to protect you, but if I have to section you off from the war I will do so."

"What does that mean?"

"I don't know, I'll put a barrier around the pub or something that should be enough to protect you from outside. But hopefully that won't be for a while."

Danú looked at the moon. "It's getting late, you two. We will talk again sometime. You should get some rest."

"Yes, I think that would be a good idea, Allōs. I'll check on you soon. It was nice to meet you, Jamie."

"Likewise," Jamie said, as he smiled and waved goodbye to Mother and Danú.

Jamie and I returned to the pub and I got back on the couch and looked at the ceiling. My mind wandered aimlessly. *I hope he doesn't think I'm crazy for all of this. What's in store for me now? Will he kick me out? Will he never talk to me again? Will he accept me?* I let myself dwell on these thoughts which only made me feel worse about myself. *Hopefully everything will be better in the morning.*

"Hey, Allōs," Jamie whispered timidly.

I sat up on the couch. "What's up, Jamie?"

"Um…" Jamie looked away and then back at me. "Can you explain what the hell just happened?"

"Of course. Do you want to talk here or at the bar?"

"Let's chat here."

Jamie joined me on the couch and looked at me. I couldn't help but feel weird about him staring at me. I felt like he was analyzing me like some sort of science project.

"What are you staring at?"

"What, I can't enjoy looking at a pretty boy?"

"Go right ahead. What's on your mind?"

"Out of everything that you told me, what is true?" Jamie asked.

"All of it. I just adjusted it to terms that a human would understand."

"Why did you actually come to Ireland?"

"The holy spirit Loreley, or Mother as the Omegas call her,

113

sent me here after I woke up from my coma. She said to find a man named Jamie O'Meara. She said that you would be a friend when I needed one most and to keep you close. And you have been everything I needed, and I hope that I was a friend to you as well."

"Al, you make it sound like you're never going to see me again. I know it's only been a few days, but I like you."

"I like you too, Jamie. Got any other questions?"

"How did you get that brand?"

"Lucifer gave it to me along with these." I ran my hand over my arm and the tattoos revealed themselves.

"Oh, that's deadly," Jamie said, as he leaned in close to me to inspect my tattoos.

"Why couldn't I see them before? Sorry, I know I'm close." Jamie sat back in his place on the couch.

"It doesn't bug me at all. You have seen me half-naked before so I don't care."

"Oh, okay. By the way, you are really cute, Allōs."

"And you're not?"

"I'm nothing special, Al."

"Well, I think you're cute, Jamie."

"Thanks, Al."

"You're welcome, but to answer your question, these tattoos are ethereal tattoos. It's a system that ethereal beings use to mark ownership."

"So, like a cattle brand?"

"Exactly. They usually hold magic power as well as a talisman to ward off something."

"What are they warding off?"

"I'm assuming my own power. I feel that Lucifer wants to isolate my powers so that Ovelth can grow."

"Ovelth?"

"He is the Xorrath king, and he is the demon who has been lying dormant in me for years, I suppose."

"What does he do?"

"He's the voice in my head telling me to…" I sighed and looked at Jamie. "I don't want to tell you, because I know I'm going to scare you."

"Does he tell you things that you would rather not do?"

"To put it lightly, yes. I turned on the Omegas before I slipped into my coma. I never was so scared. I was truly convinced that they were going to kill me."

"Wait, did you kill them?"

"Oh dear God no, but Ovelth was screaming at me to kill them though."

"Oh shit, that's what Ovelth does? That's so fucked."

"Tell me about it. He's ultimately trying to break me, but I'm not going to let that happen no matter what he throws at me."

"What does he look like?"

"He has the head of a dragon with large ram-like horns. From the neck down he has a ghostly body that tapers off into a tail. But his most notable feature is these large, grotesque hands. His hands have bony claw-like fingers that are razor sharp."

"You know, you're surprisingly human for an angel. I always thought that they would be very pious and, well, no offense, the complete opposite of you."

"That life just sounds so boring. Ugh, fuck that. Some angels are but not all, not the Omegas. We drink, we curse, we have sex, stuff like that."

"Is God really okay with all of that?"

"God couldn't care less about that."

Jamie cocked his head in confusion. "What? I'm super confused. You mean to tell me God isn't this vengeful spirit that gets angry over the slightest thing?"

"Is that what you humans paint God as? But no, God isn't petty. Why do you know God as a vengeful spirit?"

"I've been taught since day one that's what God is like. Hey, I'm super tired. I'm off to bed."

"Lie here with me?"

Jamie smiled. "Okay, Al."

Jamie turned around and I wrapped my arms around him. Jamie got comfortable in my arms. It was nice to have someone in my arms again. It was not like having Luke, but it was nice either way.

"Al, what's going to happen to Earth?"

"The world will change and everyone will notice. From that point, I wouldn't know. Perhaps the world will be thrown into chaos because of the new-found truth. That's my prediction for what it's worth. I do know this – I want you and the Omegas by my side when that happens."

Jamie looked up at me. "Wait, really?"

"Only if you want that."

"That would be lovely. Hey, Al?"

"What's up?"

"How did you become an archangel?"

"There's two ways that happens. The first, you are born into etherealism. The second is death."

"Which one are you?"

"A combination of the two. I was a stillborn child and then, after I died, Mother found me and brought me to Heaven. There, she and God raised me till I was about fourteen, and they had Gabriel train me to be a fighter. Then I became a member of the

116

grand army of Heaven. I rose in the ranks and joined the Omegas but not without failure."

"What happened?"

"I'm getting way too deep with you, but Luke, Noah, and I were on a mission with three Omegas – Abigail the Jade, Zachary the Sapphire, and Alexandria the Ivory. The long story short is they died during the mission. Luke, Noah, and I still haven't lived that down. We didn't strategize well enough, and we were inexperienced, more importantly. So, they were killed by three generals of Lucifer's army. However, Luke, Noah, and I rose to the challenge and completed the mission. After that, we were up for serious consideration to become an Omega. Then a few years later, I was inducted, then Noah, then, most recently, Luke."

"How recently was Luke inducted?"

"Months ago."

"Holy shit. So war really does exist in Heaven, huh?"

"Yeah," I said, as I hugged Jamie closely.

"You okay?"

"Yeah, talking about my past hurts."

"I've heard about Noah, but who's Luke?"

"What do you want to know?"

"Whatever you want to tell me."

"Luke the White is twenty-one years old. He's the youngest out of the Omegas. He's my height, with flawless porcelain skin, big green eyes, and short snow-white hair."

"White hair?"

"Yeah. He's had it for as long as I can remember."

"Really? How did he get to Heaven?"

I sighed. "His story is a sad one. He killed himself when he was fourteen. Mother introduced me to him and we have been friends ever since. He was a basket case when I met him. He was

117

a victim of abuse and neglect. Noah really helped him through that pain, and Luke then started showing his true colors. He's so bubbly and happy – he's like a puppy in that way. However, he's much smarter and a lot less innocent than he gives off. He's seen some shit in his life."

"Wow, I'm sorry to hear that. What's Noah's story?"

"Physical abuse as a kid and a teen and then he killed himself. Then Mother introduced him to me and we became friends. Then Luke came into the picture a year after that and we've been inseparable ever since."

"Are all of the archangels' stories that sad?"

"No, just Luke and Noah's."

"Hey, I'm tired. I'm probably going to head to bed."

"Can you stay with me for a while longer?"

"You okay?"

"No. I'm scared about what is to come and having you here is nice."

"I might fall asleep on you, but if you're okay with that, then sure."

"No, don't worry. I like the company."

Jamie got comfortable, as did I. I began to drift into my thoughts.

"You're going to lose Jamie, so I suggest not getting attached to him," Ovelth whispered deep in the back of my head. I ignored Ovelth and tried to focus on the present. "You know I'm right. You feel it just as much as I do, Allōs."

I couldn't help but feel that Ovelth was right about that. I focused on holding Jamie. Ovelth cackled as he appeared in front of me.

"You know I'm right, Allōs."

"Perhaps, but that is to be seen."

"So this is Jamie?" Ovelth spread his crooked hand and hovered over Jamie.

"Don't touch him," I said calmly.

"Or else what? You can't kill me."

"No, but if you touch him, I will try my best to kill you."

He gave me a wicked smile, revealing his razor-sharp teeth.

"Away with you, Ovelth. I'm not in the mood."

My brand started to burn and glow brighter than I'd seen. I did my best not to disturb Jamie. I gritted my teeth and endured the pain.

"Is that the best you got?" I said, as I felt my eyes sting.

Ovelth grabbed me by the throat and threw me at the wall. "You obey me! And no one else! I couldn't care less if you are in the mood or not. Consider this a warning, subordinate," Ovelth said, as he disappeared.

Jamie woke up and looked up. "Al, did you fall or something?"

"Nah. Ovelth threw me into the wall. Nothing to worry about." I joined him back on the couch.

"See that's the thing, I am worried about you."

"Don't be Jamie. Just sleep," I said, as I started playing with his hair.

When Jamie fell asleep I left the couch and went to the main room of the pub. I tapped my ring twice.

"This is an open communication to the Omegas. This is Allōs the Blue."

"This is Gabriel the Gold. I read you loud and clear."

"Gabe! It's so nice to hear you! How are you?"

"Tired, but we're finally able to relax! I'm assuming you're here to call Luke?"

"You know me too well, Gabe. How is he?"

"He's a nervous wreck. Though, I have to give him credit

where credit is due. He hasn't let his emotions get in the way of his job. I can sense that he's starting to revert back."

"Oh no."

"Oh no indeed. I'll transfer you."

My ring started flashing. I tapped it twice and a ghostly image of Luke was in front of me.

"Babe! I'm so glad you called! How are you? How is Earth? How's Jamie?"

"I'm well, but more importantly I want to hear about you."

"No, I want to hear about you first."

I smiled. "Dealing with Ovelth is harder than I thought. He's getting very aggressive to the point where he came into the physical realm."

"I'm so sorry that you're going through that. I wish I was there to be with you."

"Babe, it's okay. You have a job to do and so do I."

"I know, but it's hard not being with you. I don't think I can do this."

"Why?"

"You know exactly why, Allōs."

"Is your past haunting you?"

"Yes, and it's really bad."

"Luke, always remember where you are and where you've been. You've come so far from when I met you. You should be proud of yourself."

"I know, babe, but my past assaults me." Luke's voice began to crack.

"Babe, no need to cry."

"I can't help it, Allōs."

"I know, I just hate seeing you upset. How have you and Noah been getting along?"

Luke wiped away his tears. "He and I have been getting along very well actually. He's been so sweet to me."

"I'm very happy that you two are getting along."

"Speaking of getting along, how's Jamie? What's he like?"

"He's interesting, he's charming, and he's really sweet."

"Glad you like him."

"Do you feel better, babe?"

"For now, yes." Luke's ring started to flash. "Babe, I got to go. I'll call you soon, okay?"

"Okay, babe, be safe."

Luke's image dissipated. I joined Jamie on the couch and let my mind drift off.

Chapter 10

My thoughts were interrupted by Jamie gently nudging me.

"Sleep well?"

I looked at him and smiled. "Morning. I didn't sleep but having you with me helped, so thank you."

"Did everything I think happened last night happen?"

"What do you think happened?" I asked, as I gently pushed Jamie and got up.

"Well, you're an archangel. I met the holy spirit, Loreley, and Mother Danú, and we talked about Luke and Noah before I went to sleep."

"Then yes." I felt the presence of magic. It was faint, but it was growing closer. An angel appeared beside me. I had never seen this angel before; he seemed off for an angel. He didn't radiate beauty like all angels do. He looked like a husk of an angel.

"Archangel Allōs the Blue you are under arrest for the violation of code AHI-1."

"Whose authority are you acting upon?" I said.

"Archangel Zachary the Sapphire, sir."

"What was that code again?" I asked as I got up from the couch.

"Angel-Human Interaction, clause one, sir."

"Name and rank?"

"Isaiah, and level A-1."

I started thinking; none of this information lined up. That code didn't exist as far as I knew unless the military had created a new one that I was unaware of. Not to mention the fact that he said Zachary the Sapphire.

"Isaiah, who is your superior officer?"

"Archangel Zachary the Sapphire."

I pushed my hand forward, slamming Isaiah into the wall. "I'm going to ask you one more time – who is your commanding officer?"

"Al, what's happening?"

"Stay out of this, Jamie, and keep your distance. As for you, who is your commanding officer?"

"Zachary the Sapphire of the Omegas."

I held out my hand and a glaive appeared. I held it to my side. "Who?"

"Zachary the Sapphire of the Omegas, sir. Please, I'm just the messenger."

"Kill him!" Ovelth screamed.

"I won't, Ovelth," I said calmly.

"Kill him!" he repeated. I felt my body start to ache.

"Get out of my head!" I said firmly. I felt my eyes searing with pain.

"Al, are your eyes supposed to glow like that?"

"Get out of here, Jamie! Now!"

"Not till I know you're okay!"

I snapped my fingers in Jamie's direction. Jamie's body became encased in a thin veil of blue.

I remember Luke saying that to me every time I tried pushing him away. I knew I couldn't bring myself to kill Isaiah, but I knew Ovelth would kill me if I didn't.

"What happens if I don't kill him, Ovelth?"

"Then you die," he whispered.

"I will not give in."

I heard Ovelth laugh as I felt my body crush from within. It was a horrible pain. I fell to my knees and looked at Isaiah, almost asking for help.

"Why so sad?" Ovelth said. "Do you know not who this so-called angel is? He is a charlatan. Now kill him!"

"I can't! I won't!"

The pain started to spike and I cried out. I felt the life getting drained from me. I grew weaker and weaker till I couldn't take any more. "Okay! Fine! I'll do as you wish, Ovelth." I felt myself return to normal. "Be gone, in the name of the Father, the Son and the Holy Spirit."

I signed the cross in the air and then Isaiah burst into a fiery array of blue as he turned to ash, leaving the wall behind him covered in black. I looked at Jamie and he was justifiably terrified. I waved my hand and the burned wall returned to normal. I snapped my fingers and Jamie returned to normal.

"Now before you start freaking out on me, I have a reason as to why I killed him."

"So that's the power Ovelth has over you," Jamie whispered.

"Yeah. Everything is going to be okay. I'm sorry you had to see that." I felt cold and I couldn't help but shake.

"More importantly, are you okay, Allōs?"

"Yeah, I'm fine," I said sharply.

"If that were true you wouldn't be shaking."

I didn't know how to respond to Jamie. I grabbed his hand and led him to sit with me. I stayed quiet.

I looked at Jamie and smiled. "Hey."

"Hey."

"Look, Jamie. I really wanted you to only have a glimpse of what Ovelth could do. But now you know the full scope of everything."

"So is Ovelth the reason why you're here?"

"Yes."

"Al, come here," Jamie said, as he held out his arms.

"I'm fine, really."

"Al, don't bullshit me."

I smiled and hugged Jamie. Jamie then led me to the main room of the pub and we sat down in one of the booths.

"Walk me through what happened, Al."

"I'm not sure. But I know for a fact Isaiah wasn't a real angel."

"How did you figure that?"

"He didn't radiate beauty like most angels do. I know that sounds odd, but all angels are effortlessly beautiful. He was just a husk of an angel. Not to mention that there is no code AHI-1 or any code like that for that matter. Not to mention that Zachary the Sapphire is dead."

"Do you know what he wanted?"

"I'm assuming that he wanted me dead. Are you okay, Jamie?"

"Yeah, I'm fine, Al, I promise."

I didn't believe Jamie at all.

"You sure?"

"I'm a bit shaken up, that's all." I took three fingers and pulled a fine golden thread out of the air toward me. "Maybe the timeline has some answers for me. Want to go on an adventure? Now I will warn you, we might see some demons."

"Wait! Really? I get to see real-life demons?"

"Why are you excited?"

"It's every nerd's dream to find out that magic exists."

"If you say so, then come with me. Take my hand and think of a black void with a golden thread in the center of that void."

"Okay, Al. Then what?"

"You'll hopefully see me in the void with you. I'll try to help you as much as I can." I took a deep breath and closed my eyes. I tightened my focus, and upon opening my eyes, I saw Jamie standing next to me.

"Holy shit, it worked."

"What is this place?"

"It's the beginning of the Omni Realm. You'll figure it out when we get to our destination. Timeline, who was that?"

The timeline spiked and teleported Jamie and me to an old, abandoned churchyard. The landscape was dry, gray, and very rocky. The church was dull and blended into the hills. I noticed that there were shepherd crooks planted into the ground with small silver bells dangling from the tip of each crook.

"Where the fuck are we?" Jamie asked, while looking around.

"The Omni Realm. It's a realm that archangels can travel to that enables you to interact with the past. But as for where we are, I wouldn't know."

Jamie kept snooping around the churchyard and seemed to be having a blast while doing so. "This is deadly! It's like I'm on a movie set or something!"

"Just don't touch anything."

At that moment, Jamie pulled a lever and we went falling into the ground. We landed in a dark room with cold walls. "You had to touch something, didn't you?"

"What!? It looked tantalizing! Anyway, where are we?"

"Probably a dungeon or something. Now let's try getting out

of here." I held out my hand and produced a flame. But my blue flames couldn't illuminate the room at all. I adjusted my flame and it started gleaming a brilliant white. The room was larger than I expected. Chains hung about the room while bloodstains were scattered about.

"Do all angels control fire?"

"Very few. Maybe a hundred others control this element, if that."

"Is fire bad or something?"

"Mother always told me that fire is highly coveted throughout Heaven. She said fire is power and only a few are gifted with it. The only other angel I can think of who has the same power as I do is Gabriel the Gold. Oh, Jamie, thanks for helping me. It means a lot. Why didn't you run when you and I were with Isaiah?"

"Because I wanted to know you were okay. Plus I was scared shitless and I couldn't run even if I wanted to. Al, look!" Jamie pointed to the right corner of the room. It was covered in blood.

I walked over and ran my finger through the stain. It was still wet. To the left of the stain two bloody handprints were visible. It looked like the hands were pulled away judging by the streak marks.

I said, "What the fuck is this place? Whatever it is, it reeks of demon." I felt something was off; there was no heat signature whatsoever. I couldn't make sense of it. I put my palm to the wall and tried blasting it with fire. I felt a shock go through me. *Strange, it's fireproofed. Timeline, what are you trying to tell me?*

"Since when did churches have dungeons? What kinky shit does this church do down here?" Jamie asked.

"Probably ritualistic sex and maybe a little sacrifice judging by the chains and blood."

"Hey, what's a church without a good sacrifice, am I right?"

"Oh for fuck sakes, Jamie, you are one cynical bastard, but I love it. Hey, Jamie, get this – this room is fireproofed."

"So? Stone doesn't burn."

"True, but why does a church need to worry about being set on fire?"

"I don't know. Resale value?"

"Perhaps. But this fireproofing is for ethereal beings. Let's head upstairs to the sanctuary and see what we can find." Upstairs, we entered a large empty sanctuary. The most noticeable detail was a large stone throne placed where the altar usually sat. This place was getting weirder and weirder. My eyes darted about the room and noticed a strange bird motif throughout the sanctuary. They looked like deformed emaciated humans but with the head of a bird.

"I think I know where we are."

"Where?"

"I think this is the home of the Flock, and their leader is Mephistopheles."

"The demon from *Faust*?"

"Yup."

"So, he's real? Is Satan real?"

"Yup."

"You just blew my mind, Al."

"That's what I'm here for."

"To blow me?"

"Always. Check this out."

Jamie and I inspected the throne. We noticed a bird skull that rested atop the throne, but it was cocked to the right.

"You want to touch it, or do you want me to?"

"You told me not to touch anything, Al."

"Oh, now you're abiding by the rules?" Jamie threw up his hands.

"Al, I learned my lesson."

I brought the skull back to center, and the throne began to rumble. It moved aside, revealing a hidden staircase. We followed the stairs and entered a narrow hallway. It was dark and damp, and a slight breeze was flowing through the hall. Torches lined the hallway as we made our way down the corridor. I felt a major heat signature. I placed my hand on the wall and the feeling got stronger.

"There's something behind these walls. Whatever it is, it's huge."

"What makes you say that?"

"I can sense the heat down here."

"Really? It's freezing."

Whispers emanated from the sides of the walls.

"I knew there was something here. Got an idea on how to get behind here?"

"Try pulling one of the torches, Al. Maybe it's a trapdoor or something."

With a wave of my hand the torches lifted off the wall, and as Jamie predicted, the wall swung open, revealing about fifty cells on each side.

"How did you figure that out?"

"Movies mostly. Anytime there's a spooky basement there's bound to be a trapdoor somewhere. Scooby Doo will teach you that from day one."

"Scooby what?"

"That's right, you're not from here. I keep forgetting that, Al."

Behind the wall was a small room and huddled in the corner was the creature depicted in the sanctuary. I held out my hand to light the room. This creature had gray skin and was thin beyond recognition. The creature was tortured by the light.

"The light, away with it!" the creature said, as it turned away from me.

Jamie recoiled in horror at what he saw. "What are you doing here?" he said, quivering with fear.

"Abandoned and forgotten, just like the rest of my brothers."

"The rest?" I asked.

"Aye, one hundred of my brothers are locked within these stone tombs for speaking against the Flock."

"The Flock?" Jamie asked.

"The congregation that makes this church, young one."

"Who is your leader, old one?" I asked.

The figure turned into a tall, distinguished man. His hair was black and was slicked back, and he had a matching goatee.

"Mephistopheles, interesting," I said.

The creature reverted back to his true form.

"Thank you," I said, "you've been much more helpful than you realize."

"Will you free us, archangel?"

"Can I trust you?"

"We are humble servants to those who call upon us."

"I'm not looking for subjects. I'm sorry to disappoint, but I will give you this." I waved my hand and a plate of food appeared in front of the figure and every other figure in the building. "Please, you and your brothers eat well."

"Why are you showing us kindness?"

"Because it's the right thing to do."

Chapter 11

Our surroundings started to warp and fade in and out, switching between the Omni Realm and the bar.

"Al," Jamie's voice crescendoed into a yell.

"Don't worry, Jamie. We're just leaving the Omni Realm."

"Will it hurt?"

"Only on occasion." I winked.

Our surroundings switched faster and faster until we finally faded back into the bar.

"See, completely painless," I said. I looked over at Jamie, who was completely terrified by what he had seen.

"Hey, hey, Jamie, look at me. You're going to be okay," I said, with both hands on his shoulders.

"W-what was that thing?"

"That was a Flock member. I don't know what they were specifically called, but that's who they were. All in all our adventure was very informative. Are you going to be okay?"

"Most likely, but thanks for the nightmares, Al."

"I can wipe your memory if you want."

"No need." Jamie went behind the bar and started rummaging around.

"You sure you're okay, Jamie?"

"I'm fine, Al," Jamie said sharply.

I threw my hands up and sat down in a booth. I couldn't help but feel guilty for bringing Jamie on this trip. I had forgotten that Jamie had never been exposed to demons before.

"Al, how was this trip informative?"

"It showed me where Isaiah is from, who he works for, and the name of the organization he's with. The most important thing I really got from it was the name of the leader. The Omegas had a hunch that Mephisto was in charge but this confirms everything. The only question is what does Mephisto want with me?"

"Maybe he wants you dead."

"Yeah, but why? There has to be some greater motive than just wanting me dead."

"Al, sometimes in life people have really simple motives, so it wouldn't shock me if Mephisto wants you dead simply because you exist. Maybe he's working for someone and is just a pawn in a larger game that we are both unaware of."

"That's deep, Jamie."

Jamie handed me a book with handwritten words on the paper cover that said, *Cocktail Bible.*

"What's this?"

"Everything I know crammed into one book. If you are serious about working here, study this."

The moment I touched the book, I started to absorb the information immediately. I opened the book and saw Jamie's handwritten notes; the pages were filled with scribblings, diagrams, and measurements for different cocktails and how to make them. I flipped through the pages and read:

Irish Tea Party
Irish Slammer
Moscow Mule

White Russian (Vodka, Coffee Liqueur, and Heavy Cream)
Irish Coffee
Vesper Long Island Iced Tea (Triple Sec, Vodka, Tequila,
Rum, Gin, and Cola)
Tom Collins
Bees Knees
Sidecar
Dark and Stormy
Old Fashioned and their variations
Bloody Mary
Manhattan

I closed the book and asked, "Do you want me to make one of these?"

"Up to you."

I smiled and joined Jamie behind the bar and threw together a Dark and Stormy. I gently bumped his shoulder with my hand and handed him his drink.

"Oh, thank you," Jamie said as he sipped his drink. "How does this taste better than what I make?"

"Because it was touched by an angel."

"For fuck sakes. Al, I like you."

"I like you too Jamie. I haven't scared you off yet?"

"Don't get me wrong. You've scared the fuck out of me, but not to the point where I'm going to leave. Also, how many humans can say they've met an angel, the holy spirit, Danú, and a demon?"

"None that I can think of."

"I'll see you for work tomorrow at noon?"

"I have the job?"

Jamie nodded.

133

I felt so happy, I couldn't help but hug Jamie.

"You're a touchy-feely kind of guy, aren't you?"

"Sorry, I get that from Luke."

"It's not a bad thing. I like it. You bring a certain side out of me. There's something about you that makes me feel comfortable and safe."

"You're sweet."

I stayed up that night watching more movies from Jamie's vast collection, this time binging the Studio Ghibli films.

The following morning we had breakfast together and then we worked from noon until three in the morning. It was like that for a few months. During that time we got closer and closer as friends and grew rather fond of each other. Jamie taught me things about Earth that the archives never mentioned. It was fascinating what humans created here in spite of being so primitive. But during those lessons, I came to realize that humans are not all that different from angels.

One morning my nightly binge was interrupted by something rustling in the bar. I paused the movie and headed to the bar.

"Jamie, you up?"

"I'm behind the bar, Al."

"So what's the plan for today?"

"Nothing. I'm closed today. Want anything?"

"Is whiskey alright?"

Jamie glanced at the clock and back at me. "I was more referring to food, but okay. It's on the top shelf. I don't think I've ever seen you eat but two times," he said, as I poured myself a drink.

"What can I say, all I do is smoke and drink, Jamie. Cheers."

"Sláinte."

I looked around the pub in amazement. It was beautifully designed and it looked like Jamie had poured a ton of love and money into this place.

"Was this place always busy?"

"No, when I bought the place it was about to tank till I took it over. Then over a few months this place was back on the map." Jamie looked down and noticed my ring. "Tell me about that ring though."

I looked at my deep sapphire ring and fell silent. Then I said, "I got this when I was inducted into the Omegas. Gabriel gave it to me."

"What does it do? Is that the source of your power or something? Oh! Or maybe it's a communication device, or both!"

"I think you've been watching too much Marvel."

"What's wrong with Marvel?"

"Nothing. You're strangely excited about this ring."

"Oh fuck, yeah! Now that I know all of this is real, it's just awesome at this point."

"You're such a nerd."

"That's a bad thing?"

"No, but to answer your question, this ring is my armor, and a communication device as well. So you're half right."

Jamie's eyes lit up with excitement. "How does that work?"

"My armor is embedded under my skin and when it's activated it envelops me in a thick black liquid. To put it in Marvel terms, it's basically liquid nano tech that's embedded into my skin."

"That sounds really painful."

"It's totally painless, believe it or not. It's similar to sweating. I don't remember the details of putting it on though. I'll show you." I tapped my chest and a thick black liquid started forming around me and then hardened, forming my armor. "This armor also covers my wings."

"You have wings!"

"Yeah, four of them."

"Why four?"

"It marks me as an archangel. They were so painful as they grew in. Ten out of ten would not recommend it."

"Wait, you can experience pain in Heaven? I thought Heaven was a place where you felt no sorrow or pain."

"Yes and no. For the general population of Heaven there is no sorrow or pain. But for us archangels, there is – mostly because we are soldiers, at the end of the day."

"I never thought of it that way. Can I see your wings?"

"Sure." I stepped away from the bar and sprouted two wings from my shoulder blades and two from my lower back. As I stretched out my wings, Jamie stepped back.

"Why are they black?"

"They've always been like this ever since I was born."

Jamie gave me a look.

"What's the look for?"

"I've never thought of an angel with black wings. It's just odd to me."

"Well, humans are odd to me." I chuckled.

"Fair enough, Allōs."

"Well, from what I was told, I'm a very rare case when it comes to my wings. Only a handful have black wings, and they are usually angels who had experienced extreme hardships in their lives. That pain is reflected in the color of their wings, I suppose as a memento of what they've been through. I know two other angels with black wings, and that's Luke the White and Noah the Emerald. However, they don't have them anymore.

136

They haven't had them for a while. They requested that they be turned white because they hated that reminder of their past."

"Oh shit, that's deep. Hey, weird question, are you dead or alive?"

"I'm a living being. However, in the human world I cannot die under any circumstances."

"Really?"

"Yeah. I can only be killed by ethereal weapons or by magic, I suppose."

Jamie looked at me from head to toe in amazement. "Can I touch your armor?"

"Be my guest." I smiled.

Jamie came closer and poked my armor. "It's solid, yet it gives. Interesting."

"Hey, I got a question for you."

"What's up?"

"What's it like being a human?" I asked, as I let my armor and my wings recede back into my skin.

Jamie scratched his chin. "Oh shit, that's a tough question to answer. I believe being human is being flawed and understanding your shortcomings. Humans are strange beings when I think about it. We have singlehandedly created some of the best things and also the worst things. Albert Einstein said it best, 'Mankind invented the atomic bomb but no mouse would ever construct a mousetrap.' He's got a point." Jamie sighed. "I don't think that we'll ever learn though. Humans can be mind-numbingly stupid. There is a bright side – people aren't always that bad. We try to be as good as we can. Hopefully, I answered your question."

"You did. I guess you're not as bad as I thought you would be."

"You expected me to be worse?"

"Yes, but you've proven that humans are better than what I once thought. Most angels don't really care for humans. We tend to think that humans are uncivilized, truth be told."

"You have too much faith in this boy, Allōs," Ovelth said. I shook off what Ovelth was saying.

"You okay, Allōs?"

"Yeah, Ovelth is just talking to me. I have a nagging fear that he's here to stay and it's not a passing phase."

"Is there any way of getting rid of him?"

"I wouldn't know. His domain is the realm of the soul called Sêle Asparia, and that's very difficult to get to. Even if I do manage to get there, I have no clue how I would kill him from that point."

My train of thought was interrupted by a deep voice: "You cannot kill me, child." I paid Ovelth no mind and let my mind wander. Jamie noticed that I was spacing out.

"Al, you okay?"

"What?" I ripped myself back into reality. "Yeah, I'm fine. Care to watch a movie or something?"

"That sounds lovely." We proceeded to watch movies all day. Jamie took a nap. I kept the TV running to keep my thoughts at bay. Nothing good ever comes from me being with my thoughts as of late. Ovelth has been a bit more vocal than he normally is. I kept watching movies till well into the night.

Chapter 12

The next thing I knew I was being woken up by Jamie.

"Morning, Al," he said, as he gently shook me awake.

I groaned as I started to phase back into reality. It was nice not having another nightmare, but I still found it strange that I was sleeping more often. *I guess Earth is affecting me more than I would like.*

"Hey." I stretched, and ruffled Jamie's hair.

He chuckled. "Having fun?"

"Yeah. Would you ever let me braid your hair?"

"Please don't – last time I let someone braid my hair it ended up in a giant knot."

"Let me guess: Morgan?"

"Yeah, I actually had to cut my hair after that. It took me months for it to grow back to normal. Oh, I made breakfast. Want any?"

"What did you make?"

"Pancakes, the American kind. Nice and fluffy."

"That sounds amazing, but I should be fine, thanks though."

"Do you eat and I'm never around to see it?"

"No. Angels just don't eat for substance. We more or less eat recreationally. We feed off of the energy around us for sustenance."

"Ah, that makes sense now. So you're an energy vampire?"

"Basically."

"Well, if you decide you want any food, there's tons of food in the kitchen, so feel free," Jamie said, and he left to tend to the bar.

"Thanks." I rubbed my eyes and groaned again. Mother appeared next to me in her signature blue star-spangled dress. She was sitting cross-legged.

"I was wondering when you were going to show up." I noticed that mother was also wearing her golden shawl.

"I haven't seen you wear your shawl since I was a kid."

"Oh, this old thing? I just threw it on. It pairs great with this dress. Did you sleep well?"

"Last night yes, but I don't like it when I sleep. Nothing good comes from it." Mother noticed the markings on my arm and she raised an eyebrow. I felt my hearts stop. *What is she going to say? Will she be mad?* I didn't know what to think.

"Who gave you those?" Mother asked calmly.

"Lucifer," I answered.

Mother sighed. "I thought as much. Was that all he did to you?"

"How did you know it was him?"

"The demented figures are his hallmark. I'll never forget the day I first saw those markings. It was at the beginning of the Luciferian wars. I remember it started in the throne room when your father and I were addressing the Omegas of the time. We were interrupted by Lucifer barging in on us. I remember all of his skin was stained with the marks that you now bear. I remember his eyes… They were filled with rage, but beneath all of that hatred was immense sadness. From that moment I knew I had failed, not only as a mother but as a spiritual guardian. He demanded that God relinquish his throne, which, of course, he didn't. Your father quietly rose from his throne and summoned

140

his weapon. The Omegas surrounded him, then I stepped forth. I didn't want to fight Lucifer, and judging by the look in his eyes, neither did he. He wanted revenge on your father. Well, you know the story. Listen to me, reminiscing about days long since past." Mother drew quiet. She gently held my hand and looked at me with saddened eyes. "Why are you wearing them in the physical world?"

"There's no hiding these anymore. I felt bad hiding these from Jamie."

"You really love that boy, don't you?"

"I do, but nothing can replace Luke. I see why you chose him for me though. They both keep me grounded and out of my head."

"I would never lead you astray, Allōs."

"How is Luke since I last spoke to him?"

"Still a basket case but he's surviving."

"Is he getting worse?"

"In a way. His neglectful past is catching up with him."

"Is he staying with Noah?"

"He is, which is good. Noah keeps Luke out of his head."

"I wish I was there to help him, Mother. Speaking of which, when will I see him?"

"Soon, but I can't let you back unless you've tamed Ovelth."

"Is that why I was cast out?"

Mother looked as if she was about to cry.

"I had to, Allōs. I couldn't let you serve in a war with Ovelth. He would have torn you apart. If you think what you did to Natalie was bad, he would have more than likely turned you against the Omegas. I can't think about that."

"Mother, he's already tearing me apart, and he turned me against the Omegas. Mother, how do I tame him?"

"You have to fight."

"I try, but he will kill me if I don't obey him. He's nearly killed me a few times because of that."

"He isn't the king of the Xorraths for nothing. Ovelth is an ancient and powerful demon, Allōs. Here, this should keep Ovelth at bay." Mother swirled her hand and a veil of warm amber light surrounded her hand. She placed it on the right side of my chest with a quick downward motion. My right arm was covered in suns, moons, and stars in constellations.

"What did you add?"

"On the center of the right side of your chest, an alpha to balance the omega. And then my personal touch. These markings will give you power to keep Ovelth at bay. These will be your strongest weapon against him. Allōs, you haven't lost yet. I will never allow that. Do you want to know the difference between you and Lucifer?"

"What's that?"

"The difference is, you want to change, he didn't. That's all that matters. As long as you keep that drive you will never turn," Mother said, as she hugged me. I hugged her back like a scared child. Hell, who was I kidding? I *was* a scared child. "Allōs, don't let Lucifer, and more importantly Ovelth, get into your head. That's exactly what they want. For the moment they are in your head, you will begin to doubt, and that is when you will truly start to crumble. Allōs, it's time that I teach you one of my most powerful spells."

"And what would that be?"

"My silk strings."

"Mother, I'm not worthy of that power."

"I'm giving you this power so that you can crush any opposition." Mother placed her thumb on my forehead and I felt a large surge of magic flowing through me. I brought my hands together, locking my fingers, and slowly pulled them apart. Thin silk-like strings started forming at my fingertips as I pulled my hands from each other.

"No way, this is too cool. Are your strings an effective weapon?"

"Oh yes. These strings and I collected the bodies of many demons during my time. I used to spin the most intricate of webs and unsuspecting demons would wander into my trap and be sliced to bits within seconds. Allōs, it was truly a sight to behold! I remember facing off an army of fifty thousand demon soldiers. Oh, that was the most fun I've ever had. I had to summon all of the strings I could muster and swaddled everything in my path. The only other thing I remember was holding my arms to the heavens and then crossing them and wiping out the army, leaving nothing but a red mist looming over the battlefield." Mother smiled.

I found it fascinating that Mother was such a high-level fighter. I had never really thought about it. I hadn't realized this is what Danú meant when she said Mother was the fighter of the two of them.

"Now remember, Allōs, there are only three people who can break those strings – myself, my sister, and now you."

"Wait, God doesn't have your power?"

"No, he chose not to learn it. He said it was too barbaric for his taste."

I smiled. "You and Danú have the same powers?"

"Yes. However, she prefers to use a spear while I prefer magic. There isn't anyone better who can use a spear."

"Even better than Michael?"

"He looks like a novice compared to her."

"Holy shit."

"Holy shit indeed."

We were interrupted when Jamie popped up. "Al, who are you talking to?" Jamie looked up and was shocked to find that Mother was sitting next to me. He cocked his head in confusion. "Cool tattoos, Allōs. It's Mother Loreley, right?"

Mother rose from her seat and approached Jamie.

"That is correct. I am Loreley, the holy spirit of the kingdom of Heaven. Feel free to call me Mother," she said as she shook Jamie's hand.

"Hello, Mother. Would you like anything to eat? I have breakfast in the pub if you want."

"Oh, why not?"

With that, Jamie escorted Mother and me into the bar and we took our places in a booth. Jamie placed a heaped plate of pancakes dusted with a light coat of powdered sugar in front of us.

"So, Jamie, is Allōs treating you nicely?"

Jamie floundered for a moment and finally managed to say, "Um, yeah. He's really sweet and nice and he gives good hugs."

Mother chuckled. "Allōs does give good hugs, doesn't he?"

"He does! It's amazing! But yes, Mother Loreley, he's been nothing but kind to me. He's shown me things that I never thought possible. He's also shown himself as a good friend. So, Mother, tell me about you."

"Oh, well, in Heaven I serve as the holy spirit. I tend to all of the angels born in Heaven. I have a sister – you've met her, Danú. We spoke for the first time in years when we all talked on the beach."

"Why is that, Mother?" Jamie asked.

"Well, Jamie, ever since I joined the kingdom of Heaven, we've drifted apart. There was no tension between us or anything like that, but life got in the way, I suppose. She wanted to stay here in Ireland when I offered to be a part of Heaven. I asked her to come with me. I miss my sister, I really do. It was wonderful seeing her that time."

"Why don't you talk to her?"

"Huh, maybe I will."

Jamie and Mother continued chatting and during that conversation she said, "Jamie, Allōs, I want to formally introduce you to Danú. Follow me."

Mother brought us to Dunmore beach. As we approached the beach, I saw a glimmer in the light and immediately felt the impact of an object piercing one of my hearts. I fell to my knees. The initial impact wasn't painful at all, but then I felt a slow sting that grew and grew.

Mother assumed a fighting stance and summoned a swarm of strings around herself while Jamie stood there in shock. I felt a vein of blood spilling down my chest and onto the sand. I felt myself being lifted from the ground. From out of the distance, Mother Danú stepped forth. I was confused and started to feel my blood boil. My eyes began to sting and they exploded with energy and I felt them glowing with hatred. The rage started to subside. I looked down and saw Mother's markings glowing. In reflex I ignited my palms and threw a ball of fire into the sky, causing a rainfall of flames. I pulled my fist inward and the fire turned to blades that rained upon Danú. She stood there while an invisible force field deflected the blades.

"A valiant effort, Allōs."

I looked at her eyes and they were blazing with hatred.

She summoned a magnificent spear adorned with gold and Celtic symbols. Without warning, she plunged the spear into one of my hearts. Blood erupted out of my chest and onto the sand.

"W-why Danú?" I fell to my knees and broke Danú's spell.

"It's Mother Danú to you, Allōs. I shouldn't have given you your powers. Like I said before, you're a threat to my child."

"I haven't done anything to provoke you!"

"You have darkness in your heart, not to mention you are inhabited by King Ovelth! Which you are failing to contain! Why should I give you any reason to be with Jamie?" With a dismissive flick of her wrist, six spears left out of the sand and into my chest, piercing the rest of my hearts.

"Mother Danú, Allōs has been nothing but kind to me, and he tried his best to protect me. Even when he's fighting Ovelth."

"Is this true, Jamie?"

"Yes, Mother Danú."

Danú hesitated. I could barely breathe. I tried to pull a spear out of my chest, but I didn't have the strength. The only thing that I could muster was a single string that I threw and gently wrapped around Danú's neck, and I held out a hand full of lightning and inched my way up to the string. I touched the string, sending one billion volts straight toward Danú. Just before the lightning struck, Danú went flying behind me, like a puppet, and gave off a loud boom of thunder that could have toppled a mountain.

"Allōs, I suggest you not kill my sister, and, Sister, I suggest you not kill my son. I know we've had our differences but this crosses a line," Mother said calmly but sharply as she tightened her grip on Danú. Mother waved her hand and Danú's spears receded back into the sand. I gasped for air.

Danú slipped her fingers under the string and ripped it off with ease.

Mother said, "I'm only going to ask you once. Why are you trying to kill my child? Answer me, Danú!"

"Ask Allōs. He'll tell you everything." Danú gave me a condescending glare.

"Allōs, what did you do this time?"

"Nothing interesting. I took Jamie to the Omni Realm."

"That's it? Allōs, you know that only archangels are allowed there, but I'll let it slide. Honestly, I expected it to be much worse."

"That's it? Sister, he could have killed one of my children. Not to mention the fact that Allōs clearly doesn't have a handle on Ovelth. Not to mention that he exposed my child to a demon!" Danú yelled.

I was about to speak when Mother cut me off. "Allōs, stay out of this."

I backed away and stayed close to Jamie.

Mother said, "Get a hold of yourself, Danú. You have thousands of children. One dead one wouldn't kill you. Not to mention Allōs has been tearing himself apart fighting for control!"

"Oh…is this true, Allōs?"

"Yes. Ovelth nearly killed me a few times."

Danú came over and placed her thumb on my forehead. Her eyes began to glow. "So this is the power of the demon king Ovelth."

"Now do you understand the hell I've been through?"

Danú's eyes reverted to her normal eyes. "Perhaps I underestimated you, young one. Here, a token of my apology. Danú's hand began to glow and she waved it over my arm and a triskele, the ancient Celtic triple spiral, showed proudly on my right forearm. "You now have a piece of my healing power that should also help you fight Ovelth. Your mother is an exceptional healer. However, her tattoos aren't enough. This should help balance things completely. Then and only then will you be able to resist Ovelth's grip. Now, go, Jamie and Allōs. Unfortunately this morning is not the day for pleasantries. We will speak some other time."

"Yes, Mother Danú."

Jamie and I then started wandering the beach well into the afternoon.

Chapter 13

The churchyard grew eerily quiet. An ominous veil of green fog rolled in, filling the terrain. Twisted, hooded figures clad in black walked about the grounds. They were each holding a shepherd's crook with a small silver bell dangling from the tip. These creatures posed no threat to the church and were chanting something in a tongue that wasn't recognizable. They were thin and grotesque. Their beaks poured out of the front of their hoods. Their chant was deep and harmonic, which could easily lull one to sleep.

A few moments passed and the sound of large mechanisms started to echo throughout the grounds as if massive gears were churning against each other. Moments later, the church bell tolled deeply. The church doors opened and a hooded figure, presumably the head of the church, motioned the figures inside. Still chanting, the Flock entered the church in single file and assumed their seats in the sanctuary.

"Master, what is thy bidding?" asked the creatures in a single voice.

"What is the standing with the Omegas?"

"The Omegas are holding the northern front."

"How many soldiers do we have in our ranks?"

"Sixty thousand."

"Not nearly enough. We are painfully outnumbered. The holy spirit can wipe out fifty thousand in one go. We don't stand a chance. Speaking of which, where is she?"

"Presumably in Ireland."

"Presumably? You don't know? That isn't good enough! I need definitive answers!"

"My lord, I'm sorry that this news displeases you. However, we know not her exact location," the figure said. Then he burst into flames. His screams filled the sanctuary. When the flames subsided, the room grew quiet. No one dared look at each other.

The silence dragged on until it was finally broken.

"Instead of attacking Heaven, why not attack a place that is feasible?" Lucifer said, as he stepped out from the shadows.

The leader jumped out of his throne and bowed to Lucifer.

"My lord, I was able to infiltrate Heaven not once but twice! I was the one who made the initial attack, sparking this conquest! And...you suggest abandonment?"

"Yes, Mephisto. Your plan for attacking Heaven isn't going in your favor. I gave you those maps of Heaven for you to destroy it. Yet here we are, talking, and not sitting upon God's throne. So, we are going to do something that's on your level. We are going to go to Earth and conquer it. Don't fuck it up. Do I make myself clear?"

"Yes, my lord."

"My lord, if the stories are to be believed, you and all of your forces will die."

"You needn't worry, my loyal Flock members. I won't let that happen. I will do everything in my power to have us be the victors."

"So, you are helping me?"

"Yes, my dear Mephisto, but not for the reason you think. I have one target."

"Where on Earth should we start deploying troops, my lord?"

"Ireland. However, we won't send all troops immediately. We need to do this in phases. I want you to send three members to Dunmore East in County Waterford and capture Jamie O'Meara and bring him here. Do what you want with him, but don't kill him. My dear Flock, listen to me and listen close. I want each and every one of you to start planning this attack on Earth. If any of you should fail, I will kill you."

"Yes, my lord," said the Flock.

Hours had passed and Jamie and I were now lying on the beach. Jamie gently nudged me, and I woke from my nap. I opened my eyes and met his gaze. I smiled and ruffled his hair.

"Hey."

"Hey, Al. I hate to interrupt your nap, but we have to head to work soon."

I got up and started stretching. I whipped my head up and felt that something was off.

"What's up?"

"A demon is nearby." I got up and drew a series of runes in the sand, and they began to glow.

"How many demons are here exactly?" Jamie asked.

A ghostly map of the vicinity appeared and small white dots showed where the demons were. "Only three?" I swirled my hand and a cigarette appeared. I snapped my fingers and a small blue flame hovered about my thumb. I then puffed out a cloud of smoke.

"What's wrong?"

"This doesn't make sense. This map says that there are three demons here, but why so few? Are they after me? Did the Omegas fail? I suppose I could ask the eternal timeline, but would it have the answer?"

151

"Try it and see what happens, Al," Jamie suggested.

I drew a line in the air and a thin golden thread followed my motion.

"Timeline, did the Omegas lose the war in Heaven?"

Nothing happened immediately, but then the timeline spiked and I then touched the spike. Ten ghostly images of all of the Omegas appeared before me. "Oh thank God, they're still alive."

"Are all of the Omegas unnecessarily hot?" Jamie asked, as he inspected the image of Gabriel.

"Yes. The man you're looking at is Gabriel the Gold. He heads the Omegas. The one to his right is the archangel Michael the Scarlet, followed by Raphael the Amethyst, Jophiel the Auburn, Azrael the Royal, Chamuel the Pewter, Ariel the Onyx, myself, Allōs the Blue, Noah the Emerald, and Luke the White."

"Why are you Allōs the Blue though?"

"Like I said before, we're color-coded because of aspects of our personalities."

"Oh yeah, that's right. You were stillborn, hence the blue."

"Yup. What time do we have to go to work, Jamie?"

"One o'clock, it's now noon."

"Okay, cool. Who are the demons that are nearby? Are they high-ranking officials? Are they lower-level demons? Throw me a bone here, timeline."

"I'll throw you my bone, Al."

"Alright, I'll call Luke and we'll have a good time."

"You dirty fucker. Ugh, now for the part I hate most... opening the bar."

"Just give me the word and I can get this place ready for when we arrive."

"Let's go then."

I swiped my hand up and a swirling portal opened in front of us. Jamie looked through and saw the main room of the pub.

"Holy shit, this is just like *Portal* the video game."

We stepped through and the portal closed behind us. Jamie told me what I needed to do, and with a snap of my fingers, the bar was ready and open.

"Magic seems a bit too convenient."

"At times, yeah. Hey, before the night starts, I need to say this – I have no clue who will be coming through that door, so stay close to me and point out any suspicious characters."

Jamie grabbed my arm and shoved his body against mine.

"What are you doing?"

"I'm staying close to you, Al. Duh."

"You're adorable."

"Al, we should be fine. I know everyone who comes through that door."

I grabbed Jamie's shoulder and looked into his eyes. "Jamie, don't be so sure. There are three demons within a ten-mile radius. Be extra vigilant. I feel the presence of them grow ever closer to me and I'm worried that they are after either you or me. So please do me that favor, okay?"

Jamie nodded as he flipped the sign on the door to open. Thirty minutes passed and an older gentleman walked through the door. Jamie greeted him and he sat down at the bar.

"What will it be today, Mr. FitzGerald?"

"My usual."

Jamie went to the tap and poured him a Guinness and handed it off to him. As time passed, Jamie and I were chatting with Mr. FitzGerald. Our conversation was interrupted when three men entered the bar. They ordered a drink and then sat down in one of the booths in front of the bar. I noticed that something was off. Their heat signature was colder than usual. Most humans were warmer, much warmer than these three.

I tapped Jamie on the shoulder and whispered, "Hey, I think I've found our demon friends."

"Why's that?"

"Their body temperatures are abnormally low."

"Maybe they're cold, Al."

"Perhaps."

"Get this though, Al. I've never seen that lot before."

"Really?"

Jamie nodded.

I listened closely to what they were saying. It was in Aramaic. I thought this strange, because only angels and demons speak in that tongue. *This should be interesting*, I thought.

The day raged on as we served drinks hand over fist. The people in front of us still sat there. On occasion they glanced at us and then got back to their drinks. The day turned into night and the night turned into morning. Everyone left and Mr. FitzGerald had passed out, sleeping on the bar. It was three in the morning and the people in front of us were still there. The men in front of us rose from their seats and walked to the bar. They looked at me and spoke something in their tongue. My eyes started to sting and I could feel them burst with anger and fear. I looked down at my arms and Mother's tattoos were shining bright. Despite this, I felt rage boiling within me. *Why isn't this working? Isn't it supposed to keep me calm?* I stumbled around and then hit the ground.

"Allōs!" Jamie said, as he propped my head up. "What's wrong?"

"I don't know," I said. Jamie looked at me in confusion. I tried speaking again.

"Allōs, I can't hear what you're saying."

My seven hearts jumped out at me when he said that. I was completely trapped. I couldn't move whatsoever. These demons had turned my body into a prison. I was completely unfamiliar with this spell; I didn't know what it was. It was some sort of encasement spell, but it was modified to attack the nervous system. I tried getting up, but the spell they had conjured blocked all my movement. One of them walked behind the bar and grabbed Jamie. Jamie picked up a bottle and broke it over the demon's head. The demon dragged Jamie away despite his efforts. His screams filled the room as they forcefully took him away.

"Allōs, please help me!"

I can't move, Jamie. I'm sorry; they have me pinned. My rage and sadness boiled within and I burst into flames although I was still not able to move. Everything around me started violently shaking. Bottles tumbled off of their shelves as my flames raged on.

"Al!" Jamie's screams started to fade away as they dragged him out of the door. Next thing I knew, his presence was nowhere to be found. I assumed that they had teleported to where they had come from. A few minutes passed and my flames died down and I felt my rage slowly start to quell. I tried getting up and found that I could move once more. I finally managed to get up and realized that Mr. FitzGerald was still blacked out on the bar.

He popped up and said, "Did someone say something?" He stumbled out of his seat and out the door. I rolled my eyes and I watched him leave. I went outside and saw no sign of Jamie. I flew up over the bar and hovered for a few moments. There was nothing to be found. I flew around town and still had no sight of him. When I landed at the bar again it was quiet, too quiet. I sat down and placed my head on the bar and started crying.

155

"Get a hold of yourself, Allōs. You mustn't crumble now! I'm not going to let them win!" I felt someone hug me from behind and I started to calm down immediately. I felt at home; this person's arms made me feel safe. There were no more monsters in my head. I was at peace.

"Luke?" I wiped away my tears.

"Who else would it be, babe?" Luke said, as he turned me to face him.

My face lit up and I kissed him hard. "Is it really you, babe?" I looked at Luke from head to toe. I looked into his green eyes and there was no mistaking they were his. I ruffled his snow-white hair.

"Of course, Allōs, it's really me. You're shaking. What's wrong?"

"They took Jamie!"

"Oh shit. Where did they take him?"

"I-I don't know. They just took him. He's nowhere here. I have a feeling that he's alive, but barely."

"Babe, just breathe. Just walk me through what happened."

"I wouldn't know but, whoever they were, they can completely immobilize you to the point where you can't talk. Luke, they trapped me in my body and took Jamie like it was nothing. Luke hugged me close.

"I'm sorry, babe. Let's get him back, but first I need to update you."

"I don't need updating. I need to find Jamie."

"Allōs, you don't know where he is. I understand completely that you want to get him back but not yet."

"Why?"

"Because you're too raw right now. Just breathe."

I thought for a moment. "Okay, that's probably best. I love you, Luke."

"I love you too, Allōs," Luke said, as he ruffled my hair.

"God, I missed you."

"I missed you too."

"Is it just you or are the rest of the Omegas here?"

"They're all here. I just wanted to see you first."

"How have you been holding up? I've heard that you've been a nervous wreck."

"Yeah, the rumors were true. The hardest part was not waking up to you. I moved back to the tower. It was so bad, I couldn't handle you not being home. Though Noah and I got closer so that's good I— What's on your arms?"

I crossed my arms, trying to hide my markings. Luke grabbed my left arm and then pushed up my sleeve and saw that the markings went up to my shoulder.

"It also goes to my chest. The same with Mother's marks."

"Who gave you the left one?"

"Lucifer, as well as the brand. After that, Ovelth was much more aggressive and tried killing me a few times. Then Mother gave me these on my right arm as did her sister, Mother Danú."

"I have an aunt?"

"Believe it or not, yes. Apparently those two haven't chatted in a while until recently. What's going on in Heaven?"

"Nothing new, really. They marched on us but we held them back. We suspect another wave is coming and soon. However, we believe that our other forces can handle this attack. So at the moment, we're sitting pretty."

"So what brings you here?" I asked, as I poured us two drinks.

"You, babe. And let me tell you, you were not easy to find. Mother sent you to the strangest place. We searched everywhere for you, babe. Earth, it's so…primitive. Their clothes are terrible as well. Ugh, it's awful."

"I said the same thing when I came here. I'm so used to the high fashion of Heaven, though you do look really cute in jeans and a tee shirt."

"Allōs, you think I look cute in anything."

"You do though! Hey, cheers, babe."

"Cheers," we said together.

"Oh, Al, I will admit, I've done some spying on you and Jamie is very cute. But most importantly supportive. Which is a good quality, especially with what you're going through."

"Don't remind me. I just want this nightmare to be over. I feel like Ovelth and I are going to be 'good friends.'"

"Your inner demon?"

"The very same, and lucky me, I've been graced with the presence of royalty."

"Well, at least you're not a demon, babe."

"True. God, I missed you."

Luke hugged me and then kissed me softly. "I know. Now let's see the Omegas, then we can find Jamie. Do you know where he could be?"

"The only place that I can think of is the Flock."

"What would they want?"

"I don't know, but it was a very coordinated attack. I don't feel like Mephisto was behind it. It was too clean."

"Maybe someone else coordinated the attack."

"Yeah, that's what I'm thinking."

Luke looked at me with his soft green eyes. Every time he looked at me like that, I would melt. I missed that the most. I never realized how much I missed it till now. I wrapped my arms around Luke and held him close and kissed the top of his head.

"Oh, babe, since everyone is adding to your tattoo collection, here's my addition." Luke pressed his hand against my right forearm. His eyes and hand began to glow. Luke gently slid his hand off my arm. "That should hold you for now, babe, though either Michael or Mother will have to take care of the rest." I looked down and saw that Danú's symbol rested comfortably in a circle.

"When did you learn that?"

"Michael taught me. He said that it will serve me well soon."

"Thanks, babe."

"I take it that you weren't the only one who has been following my escapades?"

"Naturally."

"We've tried contacting you, but you were too hard to get a hold of until recently. So we found you the old-fashioned way. Would you like to see everyone?"

"Is that even a question?" My face lit up as I nodded to Luke and he took me by the hand and led me outside.

Luke spread his wings and I followed his lead and we flew far away from where I had been and we landed in a city.

"Where are we?"

"Galway."

"It's charming."

"Isn't it? It's a nice change of pace from Heaven. Don't get me wrong, I love Heaven, but after a while of seeing that same thing, it gets boring."

"I understand completely. To be honest with you, Earth isn't so bad. I don't get why angels hate it so much. It's not the worst place I've ever been to."

"I mean, I get where you're coming from Allōs, but at the same time, it's a cesspool of hatred, chaos, and sin. Plus it's quite dirty. Humans really don't know how to clean up after themselves."

159

Luke led me into a modern building that fit the overall theme of Heaven and we walked inside and I was shocked that the humans could mirror Heaven so easily. The entire building was very chic. The lines were clean and flowing.

"Are we home or is this still Earth?"

Luke chuckled. "No, babe, we're still on Earth. This place is nice, right?"

"Yeah! Who designed this place?"

"Some guy named Philip treacy."

"Who?"

"I think a hat designer or something."

"It's lovely."

Luke motioned me to follow him. We took an elevator to the top floor. This room was where Gabriel and Michael were staying and the connecting suite of rooms was where the rest of the Omegas resided. Luke opened the door and everyone was in the room lounging about. They turned their heads and exclaimed, "Allōs! Good to see you."

Jophiel hugged me and held me close. "I've been so worried about you, Allōs. You had us all worried sick. Especially after what Lucifer did to you! I'm just glad you're safe now."

I hugged her back. I said, "You all look so strange in human clothes."

"I know, it's awful. I prefer my armor to be frank," Gabriel said, as he stood up to greet me.

"Of course you do, Gabriel. It is strange seeing you out of your armor."

"It's nice having you back, Allōs. It hasn't been the same without you. Hell, I think even Chamuel missed you."

"Is that so, Chamuel? Well, I'm back, so you can rest easy."

Chamuel cracked a smile, which was an odd sight to see, for

sure, but it was nice to know that he cared. I was nearly sideswiped by Noah as he gave me a hug. He led me into the room and I took a seat on a couch next to him and Luke.

"Can we smoke in here?" I asked.

"Unfortunately not, Allōs," Gabriel replied. "I knew he was going to ask that, Michael, so looks like you owe me."

"Did you seriously place a bet on me?"

They both nodded.

I laughed and rolled my eyes. "Ariel, how are you?"

"Much better now that you're here.

"Likewise," Azrael chimed in.

Michael walked up to me and hugged me. He looked at my arm and noticed my additions. "I see Luke marked you, and he did a very good job as well. I have to admit, your tattoos do look good on you."

"I do have a question for all of you. Do you know where the Flock is located?"

"I think so, but, Allōs, I know you don't want to hear this, but you have to rest. We'll send a search party tomorrow morning."

"Gabriel, I appreciate the sentiment, but I don't need sleep. Plus, I don't want another nightmare."

"Allōs, just trust me on this one. You'll be fine. You'll sleep just fine."

"Gabe, I…I can't."

"Allōs, trust me."

I nodded and Luke took me to his room. "You'll be sleeping with me tonight."

"Oh damn, I really wanted to sleep with Azrael tonight, babe. I guess I'll have to settle for you," I said, as I wrapped my arms around Luke and playfully threw him onto the bed.

"You're cute."

161

"No, you are, babe."

Luke brushed my hair out of my eyes and kissed me. "I missed you, Allōs."

"I missed you too."

"Get some rest, babe," Luke said as we undressed each other. But Luke gave me a look that said he wanted something from me; he started rubbing my chest.

I kissed the top of his head as I whispered, "Not tonight. Goodnight, my love." Luke pulled me by the neck to his lips and kissed me goodnight.

I lay there for a while as the sounds of Jamie's screams echoed in my head. I pulled Luke over so that his head rested on my chest. I held up my left arm and couldn't help but think that Michael was right; these do look decent on me.

"Allōs?"

"Yeah, Luke?"

"Are you still up?"

"Yeah, my mind is racing. I can't get Jamie's cry for help out of my head."

"Damn, you really love this boy, don't you?"

"Babe, don't talk like that. You know my heart belongs to you and you only."

"I know, Allōs, but sometimes, the thought has crossed my mind – you two seemed so happy. Do you love him?"

"That's a loaded question, but yes I do. However, not romantically. I love him like I love Noah."

"Oh, then I'm sorry for doubting you, Allōs. Final question, I promise."

"Fire away."

"Did you two have sex?"

"No. I could never do that to you."

"Okay, good."

"Are you satisfied?"

"I am," he said, as he nuzzled against my chest. Luke waved his hand and my tattoos started to glow. "They do look really good on you. You should get more."

"Okay, when we get back home, I'll get some more. Goodnight, babe."

"Goodnight, Al," Luke said, as he kissed me.

I closed my eyes and felt myself being lulled to sleep.

Chapter 14

The next morning I was woken by Luke giving me a gentle nudge. I opened my eyes and met his gaze. I had missed this; I missed staring into Luke's green eyes. I ran my fingers through his hair and kissed him.

"Morning, babe."

"Sleep well, Allōs?"

"I hate to admit it, but Gabriel was right."

Luke ran his fingers across the omega sign on the left side of my chest and inspected the tattoos. "I hate what some of them represent, but damn do they look hot on you."

"You just like tatted boys, don't you?"

"No, I just like them on you."

"You're a mess."

"And you're not?"

"Point taken."

I got up and started making coffee. Luke and I showered and got dressed and made our way to Gabriel and Michael's room. I gently knocked on the door and Michael answered.

"Morning, Allōs, Luke. I trust you slept well."

"I did, actually."

"What about you, Luke?"

"It was really nice waking up to Allōs again."

I sipped my coffee. Michael motioned us in and we all sat down around the coffee table. Gabriel looked up from his papers and smiled.

"Morning, Luke, Allōs. It's really nice seeing you two back together."

"It's nice to be back together."

"Now, Al, before we go any further, you will see things that you don't want to see. What makes you think that he's still alive?"

I sighed. "Nothing, but I need to find out for myself."

"This is going to be a very simple task for you two. We believe that Jamie is being held at an abandoned church that was fashioned into Mephisto's headquarters. But be careful – it is protected by the Flock. They are much more powerful than one would think."

"I can attest to that. Before they took Jamie, they muttered something in Aramaic, and I hit the floor and couldn't move nor did I have any powers. It was just rage. After they left, I calmed down and my powers came back. I have no idea how to counter any of that."

"Did you enable your armor?" Gabriel asked.

"No, why?"

"Remember, your armor can protect you from magical attacks and any and all blunt-force attacks, Allōs."

"Yeah, I know, Gabe, but I genuinely forgot."

"Well, don't forget next time, Al. It could be the difference between life and death. Now, go save Jamie! We think we've found where Mephisto's fortress is exactly. We'll drop you there." Gabriel swept his arm up and a portal swirled open.

Luke and I walked through the portal and entered the all-too-familiar churchyard. A veil of green fog rolled in as we approached the church. We came into the sanctuary.

"Ugh, I can't see a thing in here," Luke said.

"Here, this should help." I snapped my fingers and every torch lit itself. "Why is no one here?"

"That's actually a really good question."

"Perhaps they're out?"

"But where would they be, Allōs?"

"Earth maybe? I wouldn't know."

"Do you have any idea where Jamie would be, Al?"

"There's a passageway under the throne. We can start there." I led Luke to the throne.

"What's under there?"

"A prison for the heretics of the group."

"That's fucked up."

"Yeah. They said that Mephisto is a tyrannical leader."

"You talked to them?"

"Yeah, both Jamie and I did."

"Was that the best course of action?"

"I had to figure something out, and I brought him along. Mother Danú nearly killed me for it, and I see why now."

I looked at the throne and the bird skull was centered in place. I turned the skull and the throne moved aside, showing the passageway. Luke summoned his weapon. His weapon was a plain silver staff, but the beauty of it was that it could morph into any weapon he chose. I summoned my glaive and carefully walked down the stairs.

Luke gave me a confused look as he stared at a blank hallway.

"They are behind the walls," I said, as I levitated the torches which revealed the cells. We walked down the hallway and there was no sign of Jamie.

"Babe, he's not here," I said. I felt myself shaking with anxiety.

"Allōs, Jamie is here. I can sense his presence. I know you can feel it too. Just clear your mind and you will sense Jamie's anxiety."

I took a deep breath and cleared my mind. I sensed extreme anxiety radiating through this building, but it wasn't from the prison. It felt like it was coming from deep under the sanctuary.

I said, "Come to the sanctuary with me."

We went back up to the sanctuary as the walls returned to normal. The throne moved back in place as the bird skull re-centered itself. I placed my hand on the floor and closed my eyes. I could see a series of tunnels and mazes underneath the floor that all connected to a center room.

"There's a labyrinth down here. It's strange. Why would you need one?"

"Beats me, babe. Is Jamie down there?"

"Yes, he's in the center of the labyrinth. It's probably a torture chamber of some sort."

"What makes you say that?"

"When Jamie and I were here, we fell through the ground outside and landed in a large stone chamber that was stained with blood and had chains everywhere."

"How did that happen?"

"Jamie saw a lever and thought that it was a good idea to pull said lever."

"How can we get to Jamie, Allōs?"

"There's a hatch in the middle of the room. We go down there, we get to Jamie." I lifted my hand and the pews hovered above the ground. I closed my hand and they faded into the wind. A large, locked hatch rested where the pews had been. We approached the hatch; it was larger than I expected. It was a plain piece of wood with four decorative metal plates on each side with a large rust-covered padlock.

"Oh, Luke, I forgot to mention, this place is completely fireproofed."

"Hmm, then we can't open this hatch normally then."

"There's a font behind the throne if that helps."

"It does actually." Luke took a deep breath as the air around us started to pick up and slowly crescendoed into raging winds. Luke swirled the air around him to carry the water from the font to the padlock. The water spiraled out of the font and violently crashed into the padlock. Luke cooled the air around the padlock, freezing it. He summoned a war hammer and shattered the lock into bits. With a casual flick of his wrist, he sent the hatch flying out of the ground.

"After you, babe."

"Thank you."

We went down a flight of stone stairs which leveled off into a stone room with ceilings that curved into an arch. We were greeted by a heavily sealed door that was wrapped with locks, chains, and a magic seal.

"Al, are you ready for this?"

"No."

I tapped my chest and was encased in my armor. I summoned my glaive and touched the back of it to the door. The chains fell to the ground and the seal broke. I pointed at the door and it obediently swung open. Luke and I walked into a dark torch-lit room. Our eyes widened with horror when we saw a plain stone wall blotched with what looked like ink. The room was filled with chains and smelled of blood. We inspected further; I ran my hand through the stain and it was still wet. Out of the corner of my eye I noticed the three Flock members who had kidnapped Jamie from the pub. They were still in human form, huddled in the corner speaking quietly among

168

themselves. When our eyes adjusted to the darkness, we found Jamie chained to the wall. He was badly beaten and his face was covered in blood.

"What have you done to him?" I asked calmly.

The men turned to face me and muttered something in Aramaic and then laughed at me.

"So be it." Within the blink of an eye I had one of them pinned to the wall by the throat. "I'll get straight to the point. You'll tell me who sent you to take the man who is now hanging on the wall, okay? Then I just might spare your life."

The demon said nothing, and I squeezed harder. "Answer the fucking question!"

The demon glared at me and said, "Never," as he spat in my eyes.

"Then die, all of you." I swiped up my hand and pinned all of them to a large stone cross and casually flicked a small ember at them. They burst into a dazzling blue conflagration. I snapped my fingers and in a large blue flash the demons became nothing more than a pile of ash and a scorch mark on the wall. I walked over to Jamie, swiped my fingers in the air, and Jamie fell into my arms.

"Let's get these chains off of you," I said. One by one, I broke off the chains. I knew I shouldn't have looked at what they had done to Jamie, but I couldn't help it. To my dismay, he had bruises and cuts everywhere, with blood dripping down his body. Cuts and bruises were on his neck, wrists, and arms. I was startled when I felt something latch onto me. Jamie was holding on to me for dear life.

I felt his body convulse as he cried into my chest, "Al, is that you?"

"Hush now, Jamie. We're going home. This nightmare is over now. Sleep easy." I placed my thumb on his forehead. He calmed down and his breathing started to slow.

Luke looked horrified at what he saw. "Is this him?"

I nodded. "I'll answer everything when we get back, Luke."

"Al?" Jamie was still awake.

"What's wrong, Jamie?"

"Who is that?" He was looking at Luke.

"I'll answer all your questions when we get home. Sleep now."
I placed my thumb on Jamie's forehead again and he fell asleep.

Luke opened a portal.

I said, "Not yet, babe. I have one more thing I want to do
before we leave."

"You're going to kill everyone, aren't you?"

I fell quiet; nothing mattered but getting Jamie home.
Rage and sadness coursed through my veins. I wanted to cry,
but I couldn't.

Luke said, "Al, please don't do this. This isn't you."

"I'm not going to kill them."

"Then what are you going to do?"

"I don't know...okay? I can't just stand here and let them
get away with this. Here, get Jamie out of this hellhole." I handed
Jamie to Luke.

"Allōs, I'm not going to let you be by yourself."

"I'm not going to kill anyone."

"Promise?"

I shook my head. "I can't promise that, Luke. I'm sorry." I felt
myself being consumed with bitter sadness. "Just go," I whispered.

"I'm not leaving you."

"Go!"

"I'm not leaving you alone."

I pushed my hand forward and Luke and Jamie went flying
into the portal. I swirled my hand and the portal closed.

When the portal closed behind him, my sadness and rage swallowed me whole. "Damn it! I know you're right, Luke! I know I shouldn't kill them," I yelled, "but they deserve to feel my wrath!" I burst into flames. I slammed my hand on the ground and broke the fire seal over the church. I sent a bolt of lightning that blasted a hole up to the surface. I flew above the churchyard and conjured as much fire as I could and watched the place burn. I wiped away the tears of rage and opened the portal.

I stepped into the hotel, where Gabriel, Michael, and Luke were waiting for me. Michael and Luke tended to Jamie. Michael was oddly disturbed by this; I never thought anything could rattle him emotionally.

"Michael, you okay?"

"I'm fine. More importantly, are you okay?"

"I'll be fine. Do you mind if I leave Jamie with you?"

"Go for it. Oh, Al, Luke, here." Michael handed us a drink.

I looked down at Jamie. Dried blood was plastered over his face and his bruises showed in the light. I fell silent.

Then I said, "Luke, I can't do this."

"Yes, you can. I know it's hard, babe." Luke started inspecting Jamie. He had wrapped him in a healing veil of white light. "Hmm, strange. Someone broke his wrist and nearly killed him."

"It must have been a hell of a fight then."

"There's no doubt. He almost died as well. Someone cut his breathing. I think he passed out at that point."

"That would explain the bruising on his neck. I'm genuinely shocked that he's still alive. He has an iron will to live. I feel most humans would have died at this point."

"Allōs, believe it or not humans are stronger than we give them credit for."

171

"Really, Gabe?"

"Oh yeah. It's a sight to behold. The humans are a strong race. They are flawed, but they are powerful when they work together."

"Impressive."

"Indeed."

I asked, "So what brought you guys here anyway?"

"We came here to see you. Fortunately Heaven was at a point where we were not needed. Everything has been quiet so far, so we decided to come see you. And by the way, you were very hard to find."

"Gabe, Luke said the same thing."

Gabriel looked at Jamie. "Let him rest. He needs it."

I walked over to Jamie and waved my hand over his head. A large dark cloud followed the motion of my hand. "He's completely broken, and it's worse than I thought."

"What did you expect?" Luke said. "He's just a human."

"Bite your tongue, Luke the White! He's not just a human. He's a friend."

"I'm sorry for upsetting you. I didn't realize how attached you and Jamie are."

"I know you are, babe. Don't worry about it."

"How long is he out for?"

"I wouldn't know. Rest easy, Jamie. God knows you need it."

172

Chapter 15

Luke and I went into our room and lay on the bed.

"Can we have fun now?"

I got on top of Luke. "You're adorable. And yes, we can have fun, babe. Only because you're here." We rolled around the bed for what seemed like hours and it came to a passionate crescendo. Afterward, we were both exhausted and covered in sweat. We showered and crawled under the sheets, and I pulled Luke close.

"Allōs, what did you do when I left?"

"I burned down the place."

"Al, why?"

"I needed that closure."

Luke sighed. "Allōs, you're so reckless."

"And you're not?"

"I'm not as bad as you."

"True. Hey, what did you do when we said our goodbyes?"

"Oh, well, we held back the forces that invaded Heaven till about a week ago. That's when things plateaued. I was hell-bent on finding you. I couldn't handle another day without seeing you. Though Noah really helped me through this. He's a great guy."

"He really is, Luke."

"Alright. Time for me to ask some questions about you and Jamie."

"Oh, dear God."

"What did you get up to?"

"We became closer as friends, and maybe there were a few nights that we shared together, but I promise we didn't get up to anything."

"I trust you, babe," Luke said, as he rested his head on my chest. "So what do we do with Jamie?"

"Fuck if I know, but I don't want him waking up with no one to help him through this."

"I completely agree. So what are you thinking – check up on him regularly and see how he does? Hey, Al, you still live with him, don't you?"

"I assume so, why?"

"Maybe you can keep an eye on him there?"

"That could work."

There was a soft knock at the door and we rolled off the bed and got dressed and answered. It was Gabriel.

"Sorry to interrupt, but I have an assignment for you, Luke, and Noah."

"No worries. I feel like doing something will do me some good. What's the task?"

"Do you mind if we talk here, Gabe?"

"Not at all."

Gabriel called Noah to the meeting and took his place at the writing desk in my room.

"What's up, Gabriel?"

"Allōs, Luke, Noah, there has been more activity in Waterford. We believe it is demonic activity. I want you to check it out and report everything you see. Oh, and be careful. The humans are much more aggressive than I expected, though I shouldn't be fazed. You know what humans do when they don't understand something." Gabriel chuckled.

"Usually kill whatever it is in question, right?" Noah said.

"Precisely, Noah. Now, some humans are taking this fairly well, others are not. But, the fact is, they're now aware that angels and demons exist. They are very quick to anger, so do not provoke them."

"Yes, sir!"

"Good, now get out of here."

Noah opened a portal and we stepped through it.

We were standing in front of a dark gray building. We looked up and saw in large white letters a sign that said 'Waterford Crystal'.

"Allōs, what's Waterford Crystal?"

"If I remember correctly, Noah, it's a really expensive glass company that's been around since God was a boy."

We peered through the window of the building for a moment and were taken aback by the abilities of humans. There were massive chandeliers hanging that glimmered in the light. Stemware lined the shelves and shone in the light. In the front of the windows stood large vases that came up to my hip in size. They were perfectly engraved. In one of the display cases, there was a full-size gramophone; I couldn't even begin to figure out how they managed to create such a thing.

Noah said, "Who knew that humans could be so talented? Luke, I'm beginning to realize that we've been living in a bubble."

"Noah, I'm painfully aware. Come on, let's find our demon friends."

Noah said, "Al, do you think it's the Flock?"

"More than likely. And I think I know why."

"What did you do this time?"

"Nothing major, Noah."

"Then what did you do?"

"I set the place on fire."

"Bloody hell. Are all executioners as reckless as you?"

"No, Noah. I think it's just a me thing," I said, as I smiled.

"It's nice being on a mission with just us three," Noah said. "It brings me back."

"It is nice, isn't it," Luke said.

We walked the streets and noticed the presence of demons all around us. *How many are there? Thirty? Forty? Fifty?*

"There's at least fifty demons here," I said.

"I'm sensing it too," Luke said.

Noah said, "Me too, Al. Lads, let's keep moving and see what's around. Then we can report."

Luke and I nodded as we kept walking down the street. Waterford was a very charming city, lined with old buildings. It had a nice view of the coast. I felt someone rushing toward us. I turned around and a man about my age, with a crazed look in his eye, came barreling our way. I grabbed him and surrounded my hand with energy and slammed my palm in his chest. His body went limp as I held him, then he fell to the ground. I looked at his eyes and they were black as night.

"Do you think he's attacking us specifically," Luke said, "or was it random?"

"I doubt that it was intentional. Let's find out what happened to him." I tapped his chest and lifted my hand. A crystal rose from his body. The crystal was palm size and looked like glass. The crystal was clear, but inside, smoke was swirling and dancing about. "He's human but barely." I plucked the smoke from out of the crystal and held the smoke in my palm and in a quick blue flash burned everything away.

"Al, are you sure you should be using magic right now?"

"I don't see why not, babe. Like Gabriel said, humans know that we walk among the earth."

"Just be careful. I'm not too fond of that idea especially because the humans aren't the nicest right now. By the way, how come Mother didn't do that with you?"

"The soul purification? I was too far gone due to Ovelth's grip on me. It wouldn't have helped," I said, as I propped the guy up against a street sign and stood up.

Luke looked at the ground and then at me.

"Babe, I'm fine, I promise," I said, as I held him close.

"You guys are so cute together. I missed you guys. We all did."

"Thanks, Noah."

"So what's going to happen to this guy?"

"He'll wake up soon. He'll be confused for a bit, then his head will clear up." I looked down and saw my ring flashing; I touched it and a ghostly image of Gabriel appeared.

"So what do you have for me?" he said.

"I thought you wanted us to contact you."

"What, I can't call a friend? Got anything interesting?"

"Yes, people are turning."

"Wait! What?"

"Yeah, people are turning. I don't know what's causing it though."

"Shit, this is worse than I thought. How many were there?"

"Just one."

"What did you do with them?"

"Nothing interesting."

"Look around some more then report back."

I nodded as his image disappeared. I went to our passed-out friend and placed my hand on his chest. He gasped awake.

"Who the fuck are you!?" he said, putting his hands up, ready to fight.

"Whoa, I'm not here to fight. My name is Al and these are my friends Noah and Luke."

"Are you one of them?"

"Them?"

"Yeah, them. One of those…things."

"No, I'm not. You're in good hands, I promise. I didn't catch your name."

"It's Sully."

"Pleased to meet you. Here, get up," I said and pulled him to his feet.

"Al, mind if I take it from here?"

"Not a problem, Noah."

"Hello, the name's Noah."

"You're English. Interesting."

"I thought it would give you some sense of familiarity. Come walk with me."

Sully nodded, and we started wandering the city.

He said, "You sure you're not one of them?"

"Mate, I promise you we're not."

"Then what are you!? I'm sorry…I don't know what came over me."

"You're fine. But to answer your question, the three of us are archangels."

"So everything is real?"

Noah nodded.

Sully was shaking nervously. His eyes darted about as he scanned us from head to toe, trying to find something that was out of place.

"Sully, look at me. You're going to be fine."

178

"How…everything I thought was bullshit is real. What am I supposed to do?"

"Trust us."

"That's easier said than done, but I'll try."

"Good."

"Noah, I know a better place where we can talk."

"Where's that, Al?"

"The pub."

"Jamie's place?"

"Yeah."

I opened a portal and we ushered Sully into Jamie's pub. Stepping back into the pub brought back everything that had happened that night – the screams, the rage, the sadness. I looked over the bar and saw that the bottles that had fallen off the rack were still there.

Luke sensed something was off and came close to me and whispered, "Babe, you okay?"

"I'll be fine thanks, babe. Just focus on Sully." I went behind and took four glasses from the bar and took a bottle of whiskey and joined everyone in a booth. I poured each of us a drink. I summoned a pack of cigarettes and I offered Sully a cigarette.

"You smoke, Sully?"

"No thank you, fags aren't for me."

"Fair enough."

Noah started asking questions.

"I'll be quick about this, Sully, then you can go home. Sound good?"

"Alright, what do you want to know?"

"Just a few things. I'll start with this. Why did you attack us?"

"Oh yeah, sorry about that. I'm not a violent man, I promise. This man came up to me and tapped me on the forehead and

I felt myself starting to get violently angry. I'm not an angry man. I mean, we all get angry from time to time but not like that."

"Can you describe your anger?"

"Yeah, it was uncontrollable, so much…hatred, I suppose. Something in me just became unhinged and seeing you guys just made me crazy. I felt the need to—"

"To kill us?" I interjected, and then took a sip of my drink.

"It's not like that! Something told me to attack you. I'm not a killer."

"Sully, I know you're not. Can you describe this man?"

"It was just a regular man, nothing interesting about him. He just blended into the crowd."

"Thank you for your time. You've helped us more than you can imagine."

"That's it?"

"One last thing – do you want to forget this entire thing?" Luke asked softly.

"More than anything."

"And sleep…" Luke said. He snapped his fingers and Sully hit the table.

"Did you have to knock him out like that?"

"Noah, you've seen him. He's a nervous wreck. I didn't want to panic him." Luke waved his hand over Sully's head and a small black cloud followed his hand. Luke flicked the cloud away as it dissipated into the air.

"So now what do we do with him?"

"Let's send him home." Noah placed his hand on Sully's back and he slowly disappeared.

Noah and Luke looked around in amazement at the pub.

"This is a really nice place."

"Isn't it!" Luke interjected.

I couldn't help but go quiet; I felt sadness looming over me. I tried to ignore it the best I could, but nothing seemed to help. I tried to focus on my drink but to no avail. I felt something on my hand and I looked up.

"Babe, let's get out of here. We have all the information we need."

"Yeah, you're probably right. I'm beginning to regret coming here."

"Just breathe, babe."

I took a deep breath.

"Feel better?"

"Kind of." Our rings started flashing. "Looks like we need to report."

Noah opened a portal and we stepped into the hotel room. Michael, Gabriel, and Jamie were in the room. Michael was sitting next to the bed looking after Jamie, who was surrounded by a shroud of white light. Gabriel was looking over a few pieces of paper at the writing desk.

Michael looked up. "You guys are back sooner than I expected."

"What can I say? We're great at what we do."

"I didn't forget to teach you humility, did I, Allōs?" Gabriel said, looking up from his papers.

"Not at all, Gabriel."

He cracked a smile and gestured to us to sit down. "So, guys, what do you have for me?"

"Really interesting things, Gabe."

"Alright, Luke, spill the beans."

"Well, I think people are turning and probably at a large scale based on what we were told. But that's speculation at this point. We got some really good information from someone who was turned."

"You talked to a human? I thought I told you not to engage."

"Yeah, I thought you knew that we did."

"To be honest I thought you passed by a human. I didn't realize that you chatted with one."

"In our defense, we were put in a position where we had to engage."

"Go on."

"Well, I didn't take the brunt of it, Allōs did, but out of nowhere this guy tried attacking us."

"Were any of you injured?"

"No. Allōs knocked him out before he could do anything. From that point, Allōs inspected his soul. According to him he was human but barely."

"Allōs, what did you do with him?"

"I removed the darkness from his soul."

"Luke, what else happened?"

"Well, we took him to Jamie's place to talk and he told us that some nondescript man approached him and turned him. He said he felt an uncontrollable rage and wanted to attack us, and even kill us if he could. The most interesting thing that he said was that a voice told him to kill us."

"A Xorrath? Why are they involved?"

"I really wouldn't know, Gabriel, but it makes sense for them to be involved."

"What makes you say that?"

"Well, if Mephisto is still behind this, then he's here to create chaos. Using Xorraths isn't a bad strategy."

"Noah, what do you think?"

"I'm with Luke on this one. Strategically, it's a really good idea to use Xorraths. Allōs, I mean no offense when I say this, but if you have difficulty fighting one then there's no hope for a human."

"You carry a point, Noah."

"Thank you, Al."

"Al, do you have anything to add?"

"I know this doesn't apply to the conversation, but I promise I have a point."

"Fire away then."

"When Jamie was abducted, the attack was too clean and too organized."

"So Mephisto wasn't behind that?"

"I highly doubt it, Gabe. He's too clumsy for that kind of attack. The only explanation I can think of is someone else calling the shots. He's more chaos and destruction. And using the Xorraths as weapons is too smart for Mephisto."

"Who do you think is behind it?"

"I'm assuming Lucifer, but I could be wrong."

"You're probably right. We did get intel that Lucifer was prowling around Heaven along with Mephisto, so you might be onto something."

We all heard a soft groan coming from the bed.

"Hey, Al, your boyfriend is up."

"Michael, he's not my boyfriend."

"Hey, I have to piss you off somehow."

"Damn it, Michael, you just love jerking my chain, don't you?"

"It's one of my favorite pastimes."

"What, jerking me?"

"No, that's Luke's favorite pastime."

We all approached Jamie as the veil of light dissipated around him. Noah, Luke, and I were at the foot of the bed, while Michael was on the left side and Gabriel on the right side. Jamie opened his eyes and they started wandering the room. Jamie sat up and brushed his hair out of his eyes and studied the faces of everyone in the room.

"How are you feeling?" Michael asked.

"A bit shaken up, but I should be fine overall. I take it you're one of Allōs's friends?"

"Yes, sir. I am Michael the Scarlet. The man on the other side of the bed is our leader, Gabriel the Gold. And I'm assuming you know the three at the foot of the bed."

"Pleased to meet you, lads. I'm Jamie O'Meara. And I have an idea of who that lot is."

"Perfect. Gabriel, I'll let you take over from here."

"Hello, Jamie. I know you're eager to get home so I'll make this quick. Ireland is starting to get crazy and I know how much you mean to Allōs, so I don't want you getting caught in the crossfire. So, I've decided to send you home along with Allōs and Luke. I hope that's alright with you."

"Fine by me. To be honest, I'll probably need them around. My thoughts right now aren't the best."

"Totally understandable. Allōs, Luke, I want you guys to protect Jamie at all costs, okay?"

"Yes, sir." We said in unison.

"Jamie, you ready to head home?" I asked.

"Absolutely!"

"Can you walk?"

"I should be able to." Jamie got up and limped his way toward us. "Michael, Gabriel, will I see you guys again?"

"We'll probably stop by to check on you."

"Well it's been nice meeting you."

"Jamie, you take care now."

"I will." With that, Jamie, Luke, and I went back to the bar.

*

184

When we stepped into the pub Jamie seemed off. I couldn't blame him. He quietly went behind the bar and started consolidating the glasses and liquor and cleaning up. He picked up the pieces of the broken bottle and threw them out.

"Al, is he going to be okay?" Luke whispered.

"He's tougher than he looks, but give him some time. He'll pull through. Babe, I hope you're okay with Jamie and me being so close."

"Allōs, if I wasn't, I'd tell you. You're allowed to have friends."

"I just wanted to double-check."

"I'm not jealous, I promise. You've given me all the things I wanted to know."

"Fuck!"

Luke and I whipped our heads round toward the bar and saw Jamie holding his wrist. His hand had started bleeding. I was about to take a step and was stopped.

"I'm fine, Al," Jamie said sharply.

I was taken aback by this. Jamie had never been that sharp with me, though I couldn't blame him.

"Sorry, Al, that's not fair to you," Jamie said, as he wiped away the blood.

"You're fine. May I see your hand?"

Jamie held out his hand. I ran my finger over his cut, and it slowly started disappearing.

"Do you want anything to eat, Jamie?"

"Sure, though we should get to the café soon. I reckon it's about to close."

We headed to the café and sat down. Jamie was understandably quiet. He kept to himself. I noticed that every so often he glanced at the door.

"Jamie, you're completely safe with us."

"Al, with all due respect, I don't feel that way. Remember what they did to you?"

"Don't remind me. But I know how to fight them now."

"I don't think that will make a difference. Al, I know you mean well, but seeing you powerless like that really freaked me out. How do I know that's not going to happen again?"

"I'm not going to let it happen."

"How can I trust that?"

"Because I'm not going to let anything happen to you again. I came back for you, didn't I?"

Jamie went quiet and gathered his thoughts. "You did. I'm so happy that you did. And I'm not upset about that. I'm just shaken that an archangel can get stripped of their powers."

"I'm just as shaken about that as well, Jamie."

"Really?"

"Yes, watching that really hurt, and I'm going to do everything I can to keep you safe."

"Al, you're an amazing guy. You know that, right?"

"I try."

"How did you find me?"

"I had a hunch that you would be with the Flock."

"Well, I'm glad to be back home. Thank you so much, guys. Oh by the way, Luke, you're way cuter in person."

"Isn't he?"

"He is."

"Oi, Jamie! Where have you—" Morgan sensed something was off. "What happened? Did he break your heart or something?" Morgan said, as she gestured to me.

"No, it's not that. I don't want to talk about it. I'll call you later and we can talk about it."

186

"Okay, Jamie. What do you boys want?"

"Three of my usual."

"Absolutely." Morgan went off to fetch our food and we chatted for a bit, but it was all fluff. We ate in silence for the most part. I could tell Jamie was completely torn apart. I hated seeing him like that. Jamie flagged down Morgan and we paid the tab and went back to the pub.

Jamie said, "Lads, I'll be in my room if you need me."

Luke and I cuddled on the couch.

"I'll give him twenty minutes before he comes out, Al. What do you think?"

"I'll give him ten."

187

Chapter 16

Months passed and Jamie, Luke, and I kept up the bar. Jamie wasn't the same; he had settled down into depression. The lovable nerd that I knew and loved was gone. The light was out of his eyes. He didn't joke as much, or laugh as much. Most nights we spent together consisted of us watching movies and him pouring out his soul to Luke and me.

"Al, I just feel empty. Will this go away?"

"In due time, Jamie, in due time. Give it a year or so. But even then, you'll still feel the grip of trauma."

"You sound as if you've dealt with this before."

"I've experienced some trauma in my life."

Jamie lifted his head from my lap and looked me deep in the eyes. "Who would have guessed?"

"Believe it or not, us angels have seen some shit."

"I'm so sorry, Al."

"Even when you're broken, you still comfort me. You will make a worthy angel someday."

"I told you I don't believe in religion."

Luke and I busted out laughing.

"What's so funny?"

"You expect us to believe that you still don't believe. It's kind of hard to ignore the proof now."

Jamie stopped dead in his tracks. "You both can fuck right off." He smiled.

"It's good to see you smile, Jamie."

"It's nice to smile again."

"Keep thinking that way and hold on to anything that keeps you moving forward, be that a song, a piece of art, a book… You get my point."

"I'll try that, Al. And to answer your religion thing, I've steered away from religion because of the rules and what not."

"I'm honestly shocked that humans are so far off the mark," Luke chimed in. "Ugh, that's not at all what God wants. He doesn't care as long as you just accept him into your heart. That's literally it. It's not that hard."

"Luke, I know you're upset, but humans will never know that till they get to Heaven's gates," Jamie said.

"Heaven doesn't have gates."

"Wait, what? It doesn't?"

"Nope. It's basically like Earth but cleaner, more intelligent, and there's peace among men."

"So, paradise?"

"Exactly. Plus it has a futuristic flair. Well, the city does anyway."

"Luke, that's amazing!"

My ring along with Luke's started flashing.

"What do they want?" I tapped my ring and a ghostly image of Gabriel appeared in front of us.

"Allōs, Luke, report to the Omegas as soon as possible. It's urgent."

"Yes, sir. I'm sorry, Jamie, but I have to go. Are you going to be okay while we're gone?"

"I should be, Al."

I snapped my fingers and a portal opened up on the wall and I stepped through and entered Gabriel's suite.

"What's going on?"

Gabriel poured a drink and handed it to me before he spoke. "There has been rampant demonic activity, and it's not just here, Allōs, it's everywhere. It's in England, Scotland, Belgium, the Netherlands, and Denmark as of now. I have a bad feeling that most of the activity is coming from here in Ireland. I have no idea what's going on, but something is brewing and on a massive scale."

"Holy shit," I said, as I sipped my drink.

"We believe that these demons are planning on wiping out humanity."

"That's an undertaking. Let me guess—Mephisto?"

"Yeah, it's Mephisto." Gabriel played with his long golden hair while deep in thought.

"So, Gabriel, is this it for humanity? Is the world ending?"

"Not if we have anything to say about it, Luke."

"Is it just the Omegas fighting this war or do we have backup?"

"We'll hopefully have backup around the world, but over here, it's just the Omegas. Fortunately we do have Mother on our side."

"Well, that's good. Where is everyone else?"

"They are in the countries I mentioned. I would have sent you guys too, but you need to take care of Jamie."

"Where is Lucifer in all of this?"

"Probably taking a back seat. I couldn't imagine him being interested in this, but I could be wrong."

"Gabe, he doesn't seem interested," I said.

"You know this for sure?"

"No, but I met him in a dream and he said that he keeps

everything in balance. He said that he's 'the other half' that God doesn't want to talk about. So why would he want to throw off the balance of the world?"

"Yeah, that makes sense. I say we give it a few days and see what happens. As I said before, I already stationed everyone where they are needed and I need you and Luke to keep a close eye on Ireland. Okay?"

"Yes, sir!" Luke and I said in unison.

Gabriel nodded and dismissed us.

"Allōs, do you want to set up camp at the bar?"

"Yes, I still don't trust Jamie alone."

Luke nodded and we stepped through a portal.

We walked in on Jamie tidying up.

"Jamie, do you always compulsively clean the bar?"

"It helps me, okay?"

"Fair enough."

Luke and I drew a symbol with our fingers on one of the tables in the booths and a map of Ireland appeared on the table surface.

"Hmmm," Luke said, "the largest concentrations of demons are in Dublin, Mayo, Galway, and Cork. There's only a few demons in the rest of the country. But what are they doing?"

"I don't know exactly, but they are gearing up for something." I grabbed the air with three fingers and pulled the timeline into existence.

"Timeline, what will happen in the near future?" The line spiked and I touched the spike and images of war, disaster, plague, and other things filled the pub. "So it is the end times they are trying to invoke. Luke, what do you think Mephisto's end goal is?"

"Well, aside from chaos, perhaps he's trying to push God into a corner and cause the final battle."

"So the war is nowhere near over then?"

"It doesn't seem so."

"We have to tell the others."

"I'm on it." I tapped my ring and a ghostly image of Gabriel appeared in front of us.

"What do you have for me?"

"Gabriel, I have reason to believe that Mephisto is trying to force the Rapture upon us."

"What makes you say that?" Gabriel started playing with his hair.

"I asked the eternal timeline and it showed Luke, Jamie, and me images of war, disease, and disasters, and demons ravaging the landscape. It's very worrying."

"How long do we have?"

"Not long according to where it was on the timeline."

"Well, shit."

"Indeed, Gabe."

"I should have expected as much from Mephisto. He's a crafty son of a bitch. Does he plan to attack both in Heaven and here or is he focusing on Earth? Does he realize that he can't win this fight? He's a bit cocky for thinking that, but I guess you have to be to do this sort of thing."

"Master?"

Gabriel looked up.

"Yes?"

"In case I never see you again, I want to say it's been an honor serving with you," I said, as I bowed my head.

"Likewise, Allōs. You've been a great student, friend, and brother. But we mustn't speak like this, Allōs. Remember, there isn't a battle we haven't won."

"True."

"I will see you two on the battlefield." Gabriel bowed as his image faded before us.

"So, is this the end of the world?" Jamie asked.

"Seems to be the case, Jamie," Luke said. "By the way, are we allowed to smoke here?"

"Since when did you smoke, Luke?"

"I might steal a cig from you from time to time."

"Oh, so that's where those cigarettes went. I thought you said that they were smelly and gross. What changed?"

"I wanted to know what all the fuss was about."

"Luke, to answer your question, I usually don't allow smoking here. But I'll forgive it this time, given the circumstances."

Luke grabbed my cigarettes from my pocket and took three and handed them out to us.

"I'm sorry, but I don't smoke," Jamie said politely.

"Well, you will today." Luke winked.

"But—"

"Jamie," I said, "I learned a long time ago that when Luke has his mind set on something, he'll do it."

"Ugh, fine." Jamie took a cigarette from Luke.

I snapped my fingers and a small blue flame hovered over my thumb. We all came together to the flame to light up and puffed out a cloud of smoke.

"Holy shit, is this supposed to be this good?"

"Yeah, it's from our home world. You like it?"

"Very much so. Do you guys want anything to drink?"

"Whiskey?" Luke asked.

"I'll have the same, Jamie."

Jamie poured Luke and me a glass and then one for himself.

"Do all the Omegas drink as heavily as you do or is it a you thing?"

"No, we all drink like fish."

"Are all angels as hot as you guys?"

"For the most part Jamie, yeah," Luke said.

"Good to know. Well, sláinte, boys!"

"Cheers," Luke and I said in unison.

"Jamie, you seem to be doing better."

"I am, Al. Every day is a struggle, but I've managed to hold on to something that keeps me going."

"And what is that?"

"Well, you and recently Luke. I consider you a friend and I would like to keep it that way."

"Aw, Jamie, you're so sweet," Luke said, as he hugged him.

Luke looked up at the TV and saw a very well-dressed woman sitting in front of a background. At the bottom of the screen a banner said, 'Breaking news. Mass disappearances at home and around the globe.'

"Jamie, who's that?"

Jamie turned around. "Just the local news," he said, unmuting the TV.

"Good evening, my name is Nicole Murphy and today I have very unusual and disturbing news. People around Ireland have been disappearing en masse across the country. Eyewitness testimonies state that people disappear and leave a 'ghostly orb' as the only trace of their existence."

Luke, Jamie, and I watched the news in awe of what was happening. The news showed images of buildings with 'Repent now or burn' signs sprawled about them. Chaos had broken out in the streets. Dublin was burning, and people were attacking each other like animals; it was utter chaos.

"Jamie, can you please turn that off?" Luke asked.

"Yeah, sure." Jamie turned off the TV.

Luke went into his pocket and threw something on the ground and then a ghostly map of the vicinity appeared in front of us.

"What's that, Luke?" Jamie asked.

"It's just a map. Nothing interesting. Guys, I'm going to set this map to lock onto the human residents of this town, which, as of now, is eighteen hundred people. Now pay attention – when these white dots go black, we need to start panicking."

"This is so cool!" Jamie said. "It's like something out of Marvel."

"What's Marvel?"

"It's a comic book company," Jamie said.

"You're too cute, Jamie. Allōs, Jamie, check this out. So, here's everyone on the map and here's us." Luke pointed to three blue dots on the map. Off to the right of the grid the number zero rested in the corner. Slowly the numbers ticked up as the map grew darker and darker. It jumped from zero to one hundred, two hundred, three hundred, four hundred, and then one thousand. Our blood ran cold at the thought that there were only seven hundred and ninety-five people left in this village.

"Al," Jamie cried, "I-I need to know where Morgan is!"

"If you go there, you will only find a soul left. And if that is the case, bring her soul to me."

"Why?"

"Because I want to know how she died."

"I don't want to think about that right now, Al."

"Then don't go."

"Al, I have to!"

"Do you?"

195

"Yeah, I need that peace of mind."

"I don't want you to suffer further, Jamie. I would not recommend this."

"Babe, just let him go," Luke said, as he put his hand on my chest.

I took a deep breath. "Fine. Jamie, just be careful. I don't want to lose you."

Jamie hesitantly looked at the door before taking a deep breath and leaving to look for Morgan.

"Jamie fascinates me," Luke said.

"Why's that?"

"He's completely broken and he knows that tragedy awaits him, yet he still goes."

"Babe, how is that any different from what we did when rescuing Jamie?"

Luke said, "Huh, I guess we aren't so different after all."

"I'm beginning to think that."

"What do you want with her soul anyway?"

"I'm curious to see if she was turned or not."

"Ah, yeah that would be an interesting thing to see."

Luke and I waited for Jamie's return and to our dismay he came back with a tear-stained face.

"Al, I hate it when you're right."

"I never wanted to be right, Jamie." I buried him in my arms. I felt my shirt getting damp with his tears. "Jamie, I'm so sorry."

Jamie looked at me, his eyes dull and dreary. The light that Jamie had in them a while ago was nowhere to be seen.

"I never got to say goodbye, Al, that's the worst part."

"I know. Here, let's go watch a movie or something."

"I'll be in my room, Al." Jamie started to walk away, but I grabbed him by the wrist.

"Stay with us."

"Al, there's nothing left for me."

"Of course there is. You have us."

"Al, how can I trust that?"

"Let me prove it to you. I'll be by your side, and I can promise that."

"Thank you, Allōs," Jamie said, as he hugged me. "Oh, Al, I brought back her soul."

Jamie pulled out a crystal and handed it to me. Her soul was clear, so she hadn't turned. I couldn't help but think that this Rapture was absolutely pointless. We all went into the TV room and chatted about our past friendships and remembered Morgan. We had a small service in her memory. We laughed and cried at the stories Jamie told us about himself and Morgan and what they had gotten up to. We chatted well into the night and got closer as friends.

The next morning I walked outside. The air was still and everything was silent. It seemed off to me. The strange thing was that I couldn't hear any birds. I wandered around the town looking for people, but no one was to be found.

I flew to Galway to check in on Gabriel, but no one was in the city. I sat down on the curb, summoned the eternal timeline, and closed my eyes. On opening them I was in a black void. I didn't know what to look for. I needed to know if that same thing that Luke, Jamie, and I saw last night had happened across the country.

"Timeline, show me what happened last night."

The golden thread spiked and then everything went white. When my eyes adjusted, I was standing in a large city, larger than the one the Omegas were in; I'm assuming that I was in Dublin. I didn't know what time it was. It was still dark though and it was cold. There were no people around, which seemed odd; however, everything was still in place as if people were there. I walked around and found that the bars were empty, but music was still playing. Food and drinks were still on the tables. It was the strangest sight; it reminded me of the war room in a way. People had been there but they had left all of a sudden, with no clean up, no tidying up, nothing.

The wind started to pick up to an unusual speed. What appeared to be ghosts in the sky floated above me and gave off a beautiful shade of blue. A ghost passed me and I got a very good look at it. I said, "Timeline, stop." Everything froze; I walked up and immediately recognized the ghost as a human soul. It was the soul of a woman. She was in her mid-twenties and very beautiful from the looks of it. Most souls usually take the form of a crystal; however, souls can also take a ghostly un-condensed form. It was fascinating to see a fully un-condensed soul. I couldn't figure out what Mephisto was trying to do, sparking the end of times.

"Holy shit, so it truly is the end of time." I closed my eyes and on opening them, I was back in Galway on the curb.

I couldn't believe what I had just seen. However, I felt that I shouldn't be surprised. One isn't really prepared for such a moment no matter how much you hear about it. My hearts started to ache for what had happened. I said, "You are all in a better place now, so be free, and fly into the arms of God."

I walked into the hotel and went into Gabriel's room and found him and the rest of the Omegas sitting quietly.

Gabriel said, "Allōs, what are you doing here?"

"How many are left in Ireland?"

"About six thousand. The entire world population as we speak is roughly three hundred and twenty-eight million."

"Shit, so is the Rapture upon us?"

"I'm afraid so, Allōs, but fear not, we will win the war," Gabriel said.

"He's right, you know, Allōs. Now all we have to do is wait for the demonic forces to congregate and we can then bring our forces to the table and we'll have the war to end all wars," Michael said.

"I hope you're right, Michael."

"You doubt me?"

I stood there completely flustered as he asked that. I could feel the rest of the Omegas hold their breath.

"Uh, no, sir, I'm just worried about what will unfold."

"You needn't worry, Allōs. You're perfectly capable of protecting yourself and others."

He was right. I had proven to the Omegas that I was a capable fighter and a good teammate to have. They had always hailed me for being a great fighter second to Gabriel. I knew I was capable of protecting myself and others, but it was Jamie I was worried about. How was he supposed to protect himself? How would he avoid this battle? Would he die? What would I do if he died? I didn't want at all to think of these things.

"You okay, Allōs? You look very worried," Jophiel said, as she sipped on a drink.

"Nothing I can't bounce back from."

Jophiel could easily sense that I was thinking about Jamie and how I needed to protect him. However, based on her look, I knew that she was going to tell me to focus on myself and then help others.

"Allōs," she said, "I know that you're worried about Jamie, but just focus on what is here and now and then everything you need to do will become clear."

199

"Thanks, Jophiel." We hugged. Gabriel offered me a drink and we stayed there till ten at night talking quietly among ourselves. Gabriel chimed in.

"Allōs, I hate to rain on your parade, but I need you to get back to Luke and Jamie. We will call you when you are needed and don't leave your post next time unless we give you permission."

"Yes, sir," I said, as I bowed and stepped through a portal and into the bar.

Jamie was behind the bar and Luke was pacing around the place nervously.

"Hey, Al, you were gone all day. Where were you off to?" Jamie asked as he came out from behind the bar.

"Just took a stroll around town. Turns out that we are the only ones in this town. Also, I have news for both of you and you'll probably need to sit down."

Luke and Jamie plopped themselves to the floor and sat cross-legged, propping up their heads with their arms on their knees. They looked up at me with curious eyes.

"You guys are such dorks," I said, as I joined them on the floor. Luke and Jamie chuckled. "Guys, there's no easy way of putting this, but…" I fell silent; I felt a wave of sadness hit me.

"Babe, what's wrong?"

"It's what we witnessed last night. It didn't just happen here. It was all across the world."

"Al, what's the population now?" Jamie asked.

"Only three hundred and twenty-eight million, Jamie." I felt my blood run cold after I said that. The conversation stuttered into silence. Then Luke spoke up.

"How do you know this?"

"I went to the Omni Realm and saw everything for myself,

Luke. I double-checked with Gabriel and he confirmed everything. It was fascinating and quite beautiful to see actually. The amount of souls that filled the night sky and the way they glowed was really pretty. But this is the end times and there's no escaping it."

"When do you suppose the battle will begin?"

"I have no clue, babe, and I can't say where it will be either. Perhaps Cork or Galway."

"Why those places Al?" Jamie asked.

"That's where the largest concentrations of demons are. I believe that they are going to merge soon and then hit Galway first to try to wipe out Gabriel and Michael, then us, which will cause all of the Omegas to rally to us, and the battle will commence. I have a strong hunch that it might unfold that way."

"What if they attack like they did in Heaven?"

"Luke, it's a thought, but I can't say for certain."

"Babe, it's a bit early but I think we should all get some sleep. I feel like this is the only time we'll have to get a full night's rest before this battle," Luke said, as he led me to the TV room.

"Don't fuck too loudly tonight, okay?"

I laughed. "Okay, Jamie."

I led Luke to the TV room and we got onto the floor and cuddled with one another and fell asleep.

In the dream I had that night, I found myself in the same church with Lucifer…

"How's it been, Allōs? Hope you've been well."

In a quick motion I surrounded myself in Mother's strings, waiting for Lucifer to make a move.

"I'm not here to fight you," Lucifer said. "That's for another day, my dear. And congratulations on being pathetic enough to have Mother gift you her most powerful weapon."

"What does that mean?"

"Please, you're not even strong enough to ward off Ovelth!"

"I almost died doing that."

"Exactly, if you were strong enough, you would have either killed the Xorrath king or died!" My anger surged.

"Kill him, Allōs!" Ovelth screamed. For the first time, Ovelth had a good idea. In the blink of an eye I grabbed Lucifer by the throat and had him pinned against the wall. I tightened the strings around his throat, causing him to bleed. I set fire to the strings and Lucifer wailed in pain. I threw him into the pews and let the strings dissipate.

"What do you want with me?"

Lucifer stood up and brushed himself off. "Where was that level of power when you were facing Ovelth!?"

I paused. I didn't know how to respond. Before I could speak, Lucifer cut me off. "It doesn't matter. We all know you're too weak to do anything about Ovelth."

"That might be so. I can take you on!" I said as I engulfed myself in flames.

"Lucifer! Get away from my child!" Mother yelled from behind me. I looked back and Mother made her way toward us. My flames subsided and I stepped out of Mother's way.

With two motions of Mother's wrist, Lucifer was slammed into a large, spiked wall. Upon impact, another spiked wall enveloped Lucifer into a spiked coffin. The coffin began to glow red-hot, and it shattered into pieces, sending shrapnel all over the church. "Allōs, he's mine now," Mother said, as strings started swirling around her. She threw out her hand and had Lucifer by the neck and then set fire to the lines with brilliant white flames. As she watched him burn, Lucifer wailed in pain at the fires of God burning him.

"Lucy, my dear, I need you to answer these questions, okay?"

Mother snapped her fingers and the flames stopped. She pulled Lucifer to her face. "Did you mark Allōs at all in any way?"

"Of course! Haven't you?"

"Yes."

"So then what do you want with me?"

"I want some answers."

"Ask away. I have nothing to hide."

"Did you place Ovelth in Allōs?"

"No, that just happened. I branded him so that he could be more susceptible to being inhabited by a demon. Ovelth was dumb luck. And I couldn't have asked for a better demon!" Lucifer laughed.

"Did you also give him his tattoos?"

"What do you think, Mother?"

Mother tightened her grip on Lucifer and started heating the lines. He winced in pain. "Yes I did!"

"That is all, dear. Thank you." Mother snapped her fingers and Lucifer disappeared. Mother turned to me. "Sorry you had to see that."

"Mother, you're fine. I promise."

"What did he tell you?"

"Essentially that I'm too weak because I didn't let Ovelth kill me. He said that if I truly was strong, I would have let him kill me."

"And you believed him?"

I didn't know what to say.

Mother held the sides of my face. "Allōs, like I said, Lucifer will do anything to get to you. Look at what he did to Jamie."

"You saw that?"

Mother nodded. "It broke my heart as it did yours. I'm so sorry that he had to go through that. It's such a horrible sight for a mother to see. I should probably speak with him."

203

"That sounds like a good idea. He's been having nightmares ever since he was rescued. On the surface, he seems fine, but I know he's hurting."

"Don't worry, Allōs, I'll take care of Jamie. As for you, I have something to tell you. This war is brewing and it will be at your doorstep fast."

"Do you know where it will take place?"

"I don't know yet, Allōs. But I do know this – we will win the war."

"How much longer till bloodshed?"

"About two days. Don't worry, the trinity will stand with you." Mother smiled.

"Oh, quick thing – was what you did to Lucifer necessary?"

"Absolutely."

"That was a bit brutal even for my standards."

"Don't worry, my son, you'll be able to see me in all my glory. It's been so long since I've been in battle."

"You seem excited for this."

"I do enjoy a good fight from time to time. Now, it's time, my dear, to wake up." Mother snapped her fingers…

I opened my eyes with Luke in my arms. I looked out the window and saw that it was dawn, but just barely. I looked down and smiled at Luke. I gently ran my fingers through his snow-white hair. I felt Luke stir from his sleep.

"Morning, Luke, sleep well?"

"Of course. I was with you."

I smiled and I started to get up.

Luke grabbed me by the wrist and pulled me to the floor. "No, let's cuddle, Allōs."

"Okay."

"Hey, let's spar today."

"Why do you want to do that Luke?"

"I think it would be fun, plus I haven't sparred with you in a while."

"I'm down. I still want to cuddle first though."

"Okay, babe."

"Hey...Luke."

Luke noticed that my tone had shifted. "What's wrong?"

"If I die, I want you to get with Noah, okay? He'll treat you right."

Luke fell silent. I felt him hold on to me harder.

"Don't talk like that, babe. I'm not prepared for that. I don't think I will ever be. Plus, I just got you back and I'm not going to lose you again! Babe, I can't go through that again."

I wiped away his tears. "Babe, we're going to be fine, I promise. I just want to know that you're going to be in safe hands if that were to unfold."

"No, I get why you're saying that, but it still hurts."

"I know, Luke. I don't ever want to lose you again either."

"Allōs, tell you what. If I die, I want you to get with Jamie. He's good for you. Mother put him in your path for a reason, so if all else fails I want you to be with him."

"He's no replacement for you though. I don't think I can do that."

"Allōs, please, for me?"

"I'll think about it, okay? As long as you consider my offer."

"Okay, fine."

"Do you think Jamie has any coffee in this place?"

"Probably."

I got up and stretched and headed into the main room of the pub. I was thrown off to hear Mother and Jamie chatting. Mother looked up and said, "Hello, Allōs, sleep well?"

"I didn't have a nightmare, so that's good. Morning, Jamie!"

"Hey, Allōs. What's up?"

"I'm looking for coffee."

"You're drinking something other than whiskey?"

"I know, right?"

"It's in the top cabinet."

I pulled out a can of instant coffee and took two coffee mugs and brewed some coffee.

"Do you guys want any coffee?"

"I'll take a cup, Allōs," Mother said.

I brewed Mother a cup and handed it to her.

"Got anything planned for today?"

"Yeah, Luke and I are planning on sparring today, probably at Dunmore beach."

"May I join?"

"Of course, Mother. What have you two been chatting about?"

"Mother and I were chatting about you and the state of the world."

"Sounds fun."

"Morning, Luke. Sleep well?" Mother asked as he entered the room.

"I did. Being with Allōs also helped."

"Likewise, babe. Oh, here's your coffee."

"Thank you. So are we going to spar or what?"

"We are, and Mother's joining us."

"Oh…okay."

"What's the matter, Luke?" Mother said. "Don't think I can fight?"

"Yeah, that's the problem. You can fight better than all of us."

"Don't worry, Luke, it's nothing more than friendly competition."

"I would love to see what Mother Loreley can do!"

"Believe me, Jamie, she can do some damage, so I'm curious what you can come up with, Mother."

"You'll have to wait and see, Luke."

Luke and I started walking to the beach.

"Allōs?"

"What's up, babe?"

"Why do you think that you are going to die?"

I didn't know what to make of that question. "My anxiety is getting the best of me, Luke. I've never fought in a war like this and the unknown is a scary thing. How are you not worried?"

"I never said I wasn't, Allōs. I'm just as scared as you are. To be honest with you, I feel like I'm the weakest link in the Omegas."

"That's not true, Luke."

"But I feel that way, babe."

"Why?"

"I'm just a healer."

"You are the third-best healer in the entire kingdom of Heaven."

"I know, but I still feel useless."

"Luke, Gabriel told me that you are a great healer second only to Michael. Do you realize what an accomplishment that is?"

Luke smiled. "I do."

"Then why are you cutting yourself down?"

Luke fell quiet. "You know exactly why."

"Luke, just remember who you are now. You are an archangel, tenth archangel in the Omegas. Third healer of the kingdom of Heaven. And more importantly, you're happier than you've ever been."

"Thanks, Allōs. That means a lot. I love you."

"I love you too."

We arrived at the beach and Luke pulled me into his arms and we rolled about the beach. We lay on the beach and just when I got comfortable Luke pulled me up. "Let's spar!"

"Ugh, fine."

Luke and I stared each other down, waiting for one of us to make a move. Luke summoned his staff and slammed it on the ground, sending a shockwave barreling toward me. Before I could react, the shockwave threw me into the sand. I got up and spat the sand out of my mouth. With a quick spin of his staff, Luke had me trapped in a gust of wind, and he slammed me into the water. I burst into flames, summoned my glaive, and rocketed my way toward Luke with full force. With one decisive swing, Luke and I were locked against each other's weapons with Luke looking into my eyes. Luke smiled and sent a gust of wind in my direction, sending me flying backward. I looped one of Mother's strings around his leg and sent him flying with me as we landed in the sea.

"Are the strings a new thing?" Luke stood up and shook off the water.

"Yeah, Mother gave them to me."

"Really nice thinking, babe."

"Luke, are you always this good at fighting or am I slipping?"

"You're slipping."

"Gee, thanks, Luke." I tapped my chest and enabled my armor.

"Oh shit, we're getting serious now?"

"Yeah, I don't think I can take being thrown around without my armor for very much longer."

"That's fair." Luke tapped his ring and his signature white armor enveloped him. I couldn't help but admire his armor. I always thought it was the prettiest out of the Omegas.

"What, Allōs?"

"Just enjoying the view." I bombarded Luke with fireballs, but he effortlessly dodged my attacks. I grabbed Luke by the arm and pulled him in and blasted fire in his chest, hurling him in the opposite direction. Luke sliced his hand through the air, sending a blade of air my way. I dodged the attack but a small piece of air sliced my cheek. I touched my face and felt blood.

"Nice shot." I looked at Luke and shot a bolt of lightning at him through my two fingers. Luke stepped out of the way and redirected the bolt and I held out my fingers as it absorbed into my hand.

"Very nice, babe." Luke smiled.

We heard two people clapping behind us. We whipped our heads back and saw Mother and Jamie.

"Luke, I don't know if I told you this, but you can absorb his lightning," Mother said, as she and Jamie approached us.

"Really?"

"Believe it or not, yes. You don't have to be a fire type to be able to do that. Though it does help. So here's how you do it – focus all of your energy at the tips of your fingers. From that point, you have a buffer between you and the lightning. The energy you stored at your fingertips will consume the lightning. You can take that a step further by not only absorbing his lightning but by firing it back at him."

"Really, I can do that?"

"Oh yes. Luke, when you're directing your energy to your fingers, pool energy into your palm as well. Your palm is the key to that attack. When you move the energy from your fingertips to your palm the lightning will be stored there till you release the energy. Now there is one flaw – don't hesitate. If you do, then that lightning will go right through you. Now, fortunately for you, Luke, you are wearing armor that protects you for that sort of thing, so always wear it when you're doing that."

"Thanks, Mother."

"You're welcome, dear. You seem tired. You should take a break."

"You're really itching to fight."

"Absolutely. Now excuse me, Luke, as I kick your boyfriend's ass."

"Go right ahead."

A bright light surrounded Mother's dress and when the light dissipated she was adorned in an older style of white armor with golden accents. She held out her palm and an immaculate golden spear formed in her grip. With the blink of an eye, Mother had me by the throat. When I realized where we were, we were standing miles away from the coast in the middle of the sea. Mother relentlessly attacked me with quick, fire attacks, pushing me further in the sea. When she got close enough, she tapped me on the chest and I went flying further into the sea. I flapped my wings and blasted fire out of my feet, propelling my way to Mother. I tackled her and crashed into the wall of Dunmore beach.

The crash shook the ground and Mother threw me off her. A swarm of strings started swirling around her. With a flick of my wrist, Mother went soaring across the sky. But I felt a pull around my chest – and Mother spun me into her web. She smirked and sent a bolt of lightning down the wire.

I fell to the ground. I stood up and set myself on fire and summoned Mother's strings around me. I sent string after string lashing out at Mother, but she deflected them with her fingers.

"Allōs, is that the best you can do?"

I mustered all the strength I could and tapped Mother's chest. She went flying in the opposite direction.

"Holy shit," I cried, "that actually worked."

Without a beat, Mother flipped back and landed on her feet and bolted at me with a decisive swing of her weapon. I blocked her attack with my forearm. We were locked together; Mother gave me a wicked smile. I kicked her off me and she landed on her feet once more. Mother effortlessly started swinging her spear around herself almost like a dance. I evaded her attacks and Mother started picking up the pace.

"Allōs, catch," Luke exclaimed. He threw me his staff.

I caught it and Mother and I entered a dance in which we rhythmically deflected each other's attacks. Mother caught my staff in the end of her spear and flung my weapon out of my grip.

"Very good, Allōs. Very good. Gabriel taught you well. And by the way, that was so much fun. You and I should spar again," Mother said. She planted her spear in the ground.

I was out of breath and I've never been so tired in my life.

"Luke," Mother said, "would you like to join in on the fun?"

"I'm good, Mother, thank you."

"Babe, she beat my ass, now it's your turn."

"Ugh fine."

I held out my hand and Luke's staff jumped into my grip. I handed Luke his staff and he walked in front of Mother. Luke assumed a fighting stance. Mother swiped her hand upward and a boulder erupted from the ground. Luke jumped up and gracefully floated back to the earth.

"Luke, think fast!" Mother exclaimed, as she shot a bolt of lightning at him.

He stood his ground and held out his fingers. The lightning

struck his hand and Luke stood strong. The lightning went into his fingers. He took a deep breath, stretched out his arm, and released a bolt of lightning at Mother.

She absorbed the bolt and a roll of thunder could be heard. "Very good, Luke. I'm impressed."

"Thank you, Mother." Luke swirled his arms around himself and the wind started picking up. He kept swirling his arms around and the wind started spinning faster and faster. The sand started to swallow everything in a raging sandstorm.

Mother slammed the bottom of her spear into the ground and the wall of sand disappeared. With one quick slice, Mother's arm sent a blade of air in Luke's direction. She relentlessly sliced away at Luke as he redirected her attacks back at her. It was mesmerizing watching two masters of the same element fighting each other.

Jamie tapped me on the shoulder. "How powerful is Mother exactly?"

"I wouldn't know, but she told me that she faced a demon army of fifty thousand soldiers and took them out in one move."

"Holy shit."

"I know, right?"

"It's amazing and yet terrifying."

"Why terrifying?"

"Wielding that amount of power is crazy to me. Also, I really don't know how to articulate it, but it's strange seeing all of this."

"You're still hung up on that, aren't you?"

"Very, Al. It's still hard to process. But I know that demons and angels are real, based on what's happened."

"By the way, how are you holding up after we brought you home?"

"To be honest, it's the hardest battle I'm fighting. Al, I feel like a glass sculpture sometimes."

"How do you mean?"

"Well, there are moments when I'm completely fine, then the smallest flick to my heel sends cracks all through me, and next thing I know, I'm lying in a pool of broken pieces of glass."

"That would explain your mood changes."

"Al?"

"Yeah?"

"I know I'm repeating myself, but will this pain go away?"

"Of course. You're just at the beginning of the tunnel. The journey through that tunnel will be hard and unkind but when you make it out of there, you will be so much stronger."

"You know, Morgan said the same thing when I told her what happened."

"Really?"

"Oh yeah. You guys would have gotten along great. Oh and thank you, Allōs."

"For?"

"Supporting me."

"You're welcome, Jamie, and thank you for supporting me. I don't think you realize how much that means to me."

"I have an idea."

"By the way, I'm curious about something, Jamie."

"Fire away."

"What did Morgan have to say about what happened to you?"

Jamie chuckled. "She didn't know what to make of it. She knew I was in pain, but she couldn't wrap her head around the whole Flock thing."

"Huh, she took it better than I thought she would." Our conversation was interrupted by Luke crashing into the sand next to us. I helped Luke up to his feet.

"Ugh, babe, I can't take it anymore."

"Weren't you the one who wanted to train in the first place?"

"Yes, but not like this."

"The point of training is to push you to your limits."

Luke rolled his eyes and ruffled my hair.

Mother's armor started to dissipate and was replaced with her signature dress and golden shawl.

"Luke, you did wonderfully. Ariel taught you so well." Mother waved her hand and a table and four chairs appeared.

"Please, join me in a meal."

We all took our places at the table and ate, talked, and drank well into the night.

It was around midnight and we were huddled around a fire that I had made, listening to the sound of the breakers slapping against the sand. Jamie went to sleep, and Luke rested his head on my shoulder.

"I will see you three in the morning," Mother said. "Try to get some sleep."

"Goodnight, Mother."

"Good night, you two." Mother hugged us and then disappeared into the wind.

"Allōs, I have a bad feeling that this might be our last night together."

"What makes you say that?"

"I just have a bad feeling."

"I hate it when you get those. You're usually right when you get those feelings."

"I hope I'm not." Luke pulled me in for a kiss, and we then lay on the sand and waited for morning.

Chapter 17

We were awakened by a massive fireball hitting the beach. I whipped my head up and saw a sea of demons in front of me as far as the eye could see. Demons were swarming everything. They reminded me of a beehive in a way. The demons were a range of different shapes and sizes. Some took a more human form and others looked completely alien. They were all grotesquely beautiful in a twisted way.

I snapped my fingers and Luke, Jamie, and I were back at the pub. I slammed my hand on the floor and said, "Anyone with ill intent either man or beast shall not enter here, so sayeth I, Allōs the Blue." A large omega sign encased in a circle formed on the floor and started to glow and then grew dull. "We should be fine for now."

We all went to the window and watched the demons swarm the place, searching for us.

I tapped my ring and said, "Come forth, brothers and sisters." Almost immediately, a large beam of light came slamming onto the floor of the pub and the Omegas stepped from the light.

"Al, I hope you didn't call us here for the reason I think you did."

"Look outside."

Gabriel looked outside and fell quiet. "Shit."

One by one the Omegas enabled their armor as we waited for Gabriel's command.

"Al, what are those?" Jamie asked, pointing to the window.

We all huddled around the window and saw a swarm of rotted dog-like corpses running into town.

"Jamie, to answer your question, those are the hellhounds," Ariel answered. "Those hounds are the most ruthless things that have ever existed. I remember them running in the streets of Heaven in the beginning of the Luciferian wars. They will stop at nothing to achieve their goal. They have hatred deep within their hearts."

Their soul-piercing wails rang through the town, making my blood run cold.

"Al, what did you do to protect this place?"

"I put a protection spell over the pub, Ariel."

"Good, that will fend them off for now. Gabriel, what's the plan of attack?"

"We have to get rid of those hounds first."

The hounds started closing in on the pub, then one by one they burst into flames of blue. The smell of burning carcasses filled the air. Their wails of pain were gut-wrenchingly terrifying. Their allies did not mourn their deaths but climbed on top of their fallen soldiers, desperately trying to find us.

"Jamie, stay here."

"You're leaving?"

"Yes, don't worry. Here, take this." I held out my palm and a small disk appeared. I tossed it to Jamie.

"What's this?"

"This will become any weapon you can think of."

Jamie touched the disk and a double-barrel shotgun appeared in his hand.

"Nice choice. That can pierce through any ethereal armor and you'll never run out of ammo, so have fun."

"Why did you give me this?"

"Just in case. You'll be safe in the pub, but in case anything gets through these walls, you have that to protect you. Now I have to go. I'll see you soon."

"Al, good luck." I nodded as we teleported out of the pub.

We arrived just outside of town and were face to face with Mephisto. I summoned my strings and threw my hands forward. Just before I could catch Mephisto, he vanished. Mephisto's army started swarming us. I split from the group and flew above the army and summoned as many strings as I could. With a decisive pull on the strings, a cloud of red overtook the horizon. In the distance, another large cloud of red mist rolled in.

I smiled because I knew that was Mother joining the fray. I summoned a glaive then surrounded myself in fire and rocked my way toward the ground. I let the fire spin around me furiously. I extended my arms and a ring of fire barreled across the landscape, turning everything in its path to ash. I could see Gabriel's gleaming gold armor above me as he beckoned me to join him and Mother in the sky. I joined the rest of the Omegas and circled around with Noah to my left and Luke to my right.

"My children, let's kill these bastards!" We were all shocked at what Mother said. "What? I can't curse? I've heard much worse come out of your mouths, especially you two." Mother gestured to Luke and me.

"What did we do?"

"The question is what didn't you do, Allōs?"

"Touché."

"Everyone, follow my lead."

Mother summoned an orb of pure dynamic energy. She opened her hands to the heavens and it grew larger. We all copied her movements as we quickly summoned our energy and they all joined, forming a massive orb. We all slammed our hands together, causing the orb to shatter and rain down on the enemies. Then a shadowy figure flew by us and within a blink of an eye blood splattered over the right side of my face. I felt a sinking feeling in my hearts. I looked to my right and saw that Luke was the one who had gotten hit. He went spiraling down toward earth before Ariel caught him. I just barely grabbed on to the end of the figure's robe and threw it as hard as I could onto the ground. I felt my eyes explode with hatred. I summoned my glaive and flew with all my might and slammed it into the figure's chest, setting fire to the blade. I looked into the hood to see who it could possibly be. The only thing I saw were brown eyes looking back at me with the most burning fire I've ever seen. I ripped back the hood and it was Mephisto.

"Good luck getting him back, Allōs the Blue!" he said, as he spat in my face. I retracted back and Mephisto kicked me off of him and summoned his weapons, two small sickles.

I saw someone join me to my right. I looked over and it was Luke.

"You okay, Luke?"

"Yeah, Ariel took care of me."

Mephisto viciously started attacking us. I could barely keep up; he was too fast. I knew if I let up, I'd be cut down. Just as I thought that, I felt a sting across my chest. I looked up at Mephisto and he was about to swing for my neck. I blocked his attack with my forearm. I pushed my hand forward and Mephisto went flying backward. Luke appeared behind him. When Mephisto landed, Luke struck him in the chest. Luke tried striking again. Mephisto then blocked Luke's attack and hooked his sickle behind Luke's neck and stabbed him in the chest. Luke stumbled back. I joined Luke's side.

I felt my eyes burn with hatred.

"Kill him, Allōs," Ovelth said. I summoned a swarm of strings and bound Mephisto. I sent as much lightning as I could through the lines till I couldn't anymore.

"Very good, Allōs! I'm impressed with your power. Now show me your true potential," Mephisto said as he disappeared. When Mephisto faded away, hell hounds started closing in on us. Luke and I stood back to back. I summoned as many strings as I could and caught many hounds in my web. With a quick pull of the strings, the army became enshrouded in a veil of red as they hit the ground. I felt the wind pick up and a few moments later Luke and I were in a bubble of air. Luke swiped his arms out and the bubble exploded outward into a large circular blade. It overtook the landscape and cut down the hound army.

Mephisto reappeared and waved his hand and the recently fallen hound army rose from the dead.

"You've got to be kidding me," Luke said. In the blink of an eye Mephisto stabbed both of us in one of our hearts. I felt strange. I've been stabbed in the past before but not like this. I felt weaker than usual.

"Al, he's mine." Luke summoned his staff and Mephisto stepped forward. He summoned another weapon; this time it was a simple saber. Within a moment Mephisto's and Luke's weapons were locked together and they were face to face. Luke pushed against Mephisto and slammed the end of his staff into his chest, sending him flying. Luke then swirled his staff and caught Mephisto in a gust of wind.

Luke slammed down his staff, throwing Mephisto to the ground, causing it to shake. Mephisto got up and sent a bolt of lightning at Luke. He stood his ground and absorbed the bolt and sent it back at Mephisto.

Mephisto leaped toward Luke and Luke sliced his hand in the air and cut Mephisto's chest wide open. Mephisto called upon two hounds to assist him as he attacked Luke. Luke effortlessly dodged his advances. However, Luke took one misstep and the hounds latched onto his arm and ripped off a section of his armor. Luke threw the hounds off him and threw me his staff. Luke took a deep breath and motioned his hands as the winds picked up. What followed was a violent storm that cut Mephisto to shreds.

He clasped his hands together and pulled them apart. Within his hands a sword made of pure dynamic energy appeared. Luke rushed Mephisto and mercilessly attacked him. It was mesmerizing to watch Luke cut down an enemy in such an effortless way. Mephisto stumbled back and then hit the ground. I joined Luke's side and looked at the defeated Mephisto.

"That was amazing! Where did you learn that?"

"Michael taught me, babe."

"Most impressive."

Luke nodded. "Come on, babe, let's join the others."

Luke and I spread our wings, and as we were about to fly away, I heard a soft chuckle coming from the ground. We turned around and Mephisto was glaring at Luke and me. Mephisto levitated himself to his feet. His injuries healed themselves and he had a burning fire in his eyes.

"A valiant effort, Luke the White. But it's not enough." Mephisto summoned two small daggers and hacked away at Luke. Luke dodged the oncoming attacks. I could sense Luke's energy and it was filled with doubt. Luke couldn't keep up with Mephisto's speed and before Luke knew what hit him, he was stabbed in the heart. Then again, and again.

I jumped in on the fight and Mephisto overpowered me and sunk another dagger into my heart. I felt the same feeling I felt earlier. My hearts started to decay faster than they normally do. I knew that the blades were poisoned but I didn't know with what. I pulled out the blades from my chest and was ready to attack.

Mephisto disappeared and the hounds started swarming us once more. Luke and I fended them off the best we could, but I felt my movements begin to slow down. *The poison must be in my system by now. Luke is probably feeling the effects now. I don't know if we can keep up.*

I closed my eyes and summoned as much energy around me as I could. I lifted my hands up to the heavens and the earth began to rumble. Luke caught onto what I was doing and followed my motions. The ground shook to the point where it could topple mountains. I brought my arms in and stomped on the ground. A shockwave traveled across the land obliterating everything in sight. I turned to face Luke.

"Let's meet up with the others." Luke nodded. I turned around and spread my wings and just as I was about to push off the ground, I heard Luke call out in pain. I turned around and Mephisto gave me a wicked grin as Luke hit the ground revealing that he had three daggers embedded in his back. Mephisto disappeared and I ran to Luke's side.

"Don't worry about me, Allōs. I'm fine!"

"Luke, please let me help you!"

"Al, get out of here! Go help the Omegas." The ground began to rumble. From deep within the ground more hell hounds started pouring out and were closing in on us.

"I'm not leaving you."

Luke lifted his arm and I floated off the ground. I was being turned around and I felt a push and I was soaring into the distance.

I stopped and looked down and saw Luke fighting the hounds but there were too many of them and they pounced on him. From that point it looked like Luke was drowning. They started tearing him apart. Luke threw them off him, but one went to his throat and Luke went down. I couldn't watch this anymore. I swirled my arms around me and I could see embers floating around the ground. I kept swirling my hands and the embers exploded into a brilliant blue and created a vortex of fire around Luke. I motioned my arms inward and the vortex closed in on Luke till he was in the center of the fire. I pushed my arms forward and a wave of fire consumed the landscape. I kept sending wave after wave to kill everything in sight. I landed and went to Luke's aid.

I could tell that Luke was alive, but barely. Luke was covered in bite marks. His armor was completely covered in blood. Luke's chest had three daggers so far lodged in his chest that the hilts were only visible. Luke's throat was torn open by the hounds.

I went to pull out the daggers, but Luke stopped me.

"Al, there's nothing you can do."

"Of course there is. Hopefully this will help." I covered Luke in a thin veil of blue fire that acted like a second skin in an attempt to heal him.

"Al, Ariel already tried to heal me. I'm too far gone." I knew that Luke was too far gone. I didn't want to accept that truth. There had to be a way to save him. Tears started streaming down my face as I looked at my dying soulmate.

"Luke, I'm not going to lose you."

"Don't cry, Allōs, not now. You have a battle to win. When the dust settles, I'll let you cry for me," Luke said, as he cupped my face.

I buried him in my arms and remained silent, trying to keep everything together. My eyes swelled with sorrow as I surrounded us in a ball of fire which burned with bitter sadness.

"Allōs, look at me and remember this. I want you to love Jamie as you loved me."

"Babe, I can't do that to you."

"Do it for me?"

I stopped and thought. I knew that Luke wasn't coming back from this and it tore me to pieces thinking about it. But Luke was right about Jamie being good for me.

"Okay, Luke, for you."

"I love you, Allōs."

"I love you too, Luke." I hugged Luke close. He held me tightly then his grip started to get looser and looser until his arms fell to his side. The flames around us burned to a blinding white and then fizzled out.

"Goodbye, Luke the White." I pulled out each dagger, stopped the bleeding, and closed his throat. I teleported Luke to the beach and let him rest there.

Chapter 18

I was absolutely mesmerized watching the battle from the pub. It reminded me of a film or something. I tried my best to follow the Omegas' movements, but they were too fast. I got up and poured myself a drink and pulled a chair to the window and watched the battle unfold. I heard soft footsteps behind me.

"Al, is that you?"

No one answered. I grabbed my gun and looked behind me and was startled to find myself staring face to face with a man dressed in a black suit.

"Hello, Jamie. Are you enjoying the show?"

"Um, who are you?"

"I go by many names, all of which are unholy."

"Holy shit! You're Lucifer!"

"Very perceptive."

"I can pick up on things like that. Care to join me, and want anything to drink?"

Lucifer took my drink and sipped it. "Thanks for the drink." He winked.

"Ballsy, I'll give you that."

"Well, that's one way to put it." Lucifer walked around the bar and noticed the symbol on the floor. "He really thinks this can hold me? I thought he was better than that." He crouched down and waved his hand and the seal cracked. I stood there, dumbfounded by how easy it was for him. "Oh by the way, I'm so sorry about what you had to go through with the Flock and all. Being tortured for that long must have been hell for you."

"Wait, how did you know about that?"

"I have eyes and ears everywhere."

"Interesting."

"You doubt me?"

"I do, actually."

"You're cocky for a human."

"What can I say? I've been around the block." I thought to myself, how would Lucifer know about what happened? So why did he mention that length of time? That's so specific. I raised my gun at him.

"You were the one who called the attack."

"I was. You really think a gun can stop me?"

"I can try."

"Go right ahead then. Shoot me!" I hesitated. "What are you waiting for? Pull the trigger!"

I closed my eyes and pulled the trigger. I heard the shuffling of Lucifer's feet and a glass shattering on the floor. I opened my eyes and Lucifer was grabbing his chest, glaring at me with palpable hatred in his eyes. Lucifer held out his hand and my gun went flying out of my grip. He caught it and effortlessly broke it in two.

He said, "That hurt much more than I thought it would."

I started to panic and I took a few steps back and then hit the wall and nearly jumped out of my skin.

"Not so tough now without your weapon, are you?"

I stood there in fear; I felt myself trembling. I started to feel myself crack. I felt that I was back at the place where I had been abducted. Where was Allōs when I needed him? I wanted to scream but I couldn't. I felt tears start to stream down my face.

"D-Don't come any closer."

"Why?"

"I don't want to die."

"Jamie, you're not going to die."

Lucifer came to me and whispered, "By the way, I can heal your pain, you know."

"Let me guess, you want my soul."

Lucifer howled with laughter. Lucifer drew a line in the air and sat down on one of the bar stools.

"What the fuck am I supposed to do with a soul?"

"Wait, demons don't want human souls?"

"Eh, souls are important, but we value servitude most. Tell you what, you seem like a nice boy, so how about this? I'll heal you and you give me something in return."

"Like what?"

"Serve me and my kingdom and I'll give you anything your heart desires. The choice is yours ultimately. All you have to do is shake my hand."

I nervously looked at him and then his hand and glanced back at him. "You'll get rid of all my pain?"

"Of course. All you have to do is shake my hand."

I couldn't accept his offer. If I were to be healed I would rather have Allōs heal me. And I like the pain; it reminds me of where I am and where I need to go.

"I-I can't, I won't. Thank you for the offer though."

Lucifer shrugged and rose from his seat. "It's not for everyone. Hey, look up at me."

I looked up and met Lucifer's gaze. He had such pretty eyes.

The type of eyes you can get lost staring into. He snapped his fingers and broke away.

"What was that?"

"You'll see soon."

"Well, that's cryptic." I felt something wet creeping down my neck. I touched my finger to my throat and it was covered in blood. I felt my shirt starting to get wet. My eyes widened with alarm. I looked at Lucifer for an explanation.

"Don't worry, you won't die, not yet at least." He chuckled as he summoned a scythe. The scythe was very plain and there was nothing special about it really. He swung his blade to the left then right and then I felt a sting going down from my left shoulder to my right hip. I saw blood go all over the bar as I hit the floor.

"You humans really do die easily! No matter, you were a waste of my time anyway." Lucifer whispered something else, but I couldn't hear what it was, then he vanished into smoke.

I didn't know what to feel. I shivered with anxiety; I couldn't lie still. I was overwhelmed by sadness. I was terrified. I had never felt so alone. I wasn't ready to face my fate, not like this. I tried to get up, but I was too weak. I crawled to the base of the bar and pushed away the stools and propped myself up and let myself die.

"I'm sorry, Allōs. I couldn't survive this. I really did love you. You were a great friend to me, thank you. I just wish you were here so I could tell you. I'm not ready to die, but who is really? And there isn't any fucking thing that I can do to stop this bleeding! God dammit!" I slammed my fist into the bar and I winced in pain. "Right, don't move, it just makes the bleeding worse. Huh, it's not like anyone is coming for me. Oh, well, it's been a good run, Jamie. I just hope I can see Allōs again. I doubt it though. Where the hell am I going to end up? Heaven? Hell? I've never believed in religion, so I wouldn't be surprised if I burned in Hell. Fuck! I wish I knew this shit was real all those years ago! Why did I have to stray from the path?" I looked down, and I was covered in blood. "Huh, looks like a movie effect." I touched the cut and it was deep. "God, why are you letting me die like this? I know I've abandoned you, but is this honestly what I deserve?" I felt myself getting lightheaded. My head started spinning and reality phased in and out. My eyelids felt heavy and when I opened my eyes I was staring at the floor. I couldn't help but cry bitter tears. "I'm sorry, Allōs." The room was deafeningly quiet. I heard the door crash down as someone shouted. I whipped my head up and saw a black-and-blue figure.

"Al, is that you?"

"Yes, Jamie. I'm here."

Allōs ran his finger over the cut on my chest and my neck. "Hopefully this should stop the bleeding, Jamie. I'm so sorry I couldn't get here faster. By the way, where's Lucifer?"

"He's nowhere to be found, Al. He left shortly after he sliced me open."

"How long have you been bleeding?"

"About ten minutes."

"I can heal you completely."

"No, just be with me. Allōs?"

"Yes, Jamie?"

"Hold me?"

Allōs buried me in his arms. I looked up and was staring at his armor. I tapped his forehead and his faceplate receded into his neckline. "There you are." I smiled.

"Jamie, I don't want to lose you as well."

I felt my heart sink. I knew he was talking about Luke. "What happened to Luke?"

"I lost him, Jamie."

I wiped away the tears from his eyes. "I'm so sorry, Al." I held him closer to me.

"Don't worry about that right now, Jamie. Just be with me."

"Al, I'm scared."

"I know."

"Will I ever see you again?"

Allōs looked deep into my eyes. "Of course you will."

"I guess I should say this now. Al, thank you for everything you've done for me. You've been there when I needed it most."

"You're welcome, Jamie."

"Al, I don't know if I should say this now, but I guess I don't have much of a choice."

"What's up?"

"I loved you. I really did. You're so sweet to me and I'm happy that I caught a glimpse of what Luke saw in you. So thank you for showing me what love was."

"Truth be told, Jamie, I loved you too. Thank you for being there for me when I needed you."

"Allōs, I'm tired, be with me till I fall asleep. By that time, I'll probably be dead."

"Okay, Jamie."

Allōs held me close. I felt myself get more and more light-headed and I felt myself fading in and out till all I saw was black.

I felt Jamie's grip get more and more relaxed until he slumped onto my chest. I rested Jamie on the floor and went into the TV room and grabbed a blanket and then draped it over him.

When I got up I saw that the bar and everything behind it was splattered with blood.

"Sleep well, my friend. You deserve it." I went outside and joined the others.

Chapter 19

"Children, lend me your strength," Mother said. We gave Mother our energy as we all melded together. There was a stillness in the air. Mother landed on Dunmore beach and ran across the water and summoned a wave beneath her feet and started sailing around the coast. Mother purified the water around her; it gave off a white hue. When she closed in on the coast, she lifted the sea level to swallow all of Ireland; to wash away anything with ill intent upon the land.

"Everyone with the gift of water, I need your assistance." Michael, Azrael, and Noah appeared at Mother's side. "Flood the coastline of every country while the rest of us will take care of the inlands. Now go! As for the rest of you, purify the inlands of every country and then meet back at Dunmore beach. Good luck to all of you."

We broke free of Mother and flew off in multiple directions. I headed east from Dunmore along with Jophiel, and we landed in an unfamiliar place.

"Where are we?" I said.

"Wales, I think. So what's the plan Al?"

"I have an idea."

"Fire away, Allōs."

"Can you transmit this to everyone else?"

"Of course." Jophiel held out her hand and a small orb appeared and hovered about her palm.

"Omegas, this is Allōs the Blue, standing by."

"This is Gabriel the Gold, standing by."

"This is Michael the Scarlet, standing by."

"This is Raphael the Amethyst, standing by."

"This is Jophiel the Auburn, standing by."

"This is Azrael the Royal, standing by."

"This is Ariel the Onyx, standing by."

"This is Noah the Emerald, standing by."

I was waiting for Luke to respond, then reality hit me. *That's right, he's gone.* I felt a wave of sadness come over me but I fought it and focused on the task at hand.

"What's your plan, Allōs?" Gabriel asked.

"Jophiel and I will place a stone cross in the heart of every capital city in Europe and Asia. I need you guys to take care of the rest of the world. Light them, and I'll take care of the rest. Understand?"

"Al, be honest. You just want to see the world burn."

"You know it, Noah. I will see all of you soon." I summoned a cross from the ground and touched it. The cross condensed into a small orb. I set the orb ablaze and swiped my hand to the right; it went flying into the distance. Jophiel and I got to work making cross after cross and sending them to their proper destinations.

"Well, that should cover Europe and Asia. Jophiel, let's head to London and finish this."

Jophiel and I teleported to Westminster in the heart of London and were met with a large stone cross that was blazing blue. All throughout the city demons were swarming everything like mindless bees.

"Allōs, let's get this done with. I can't stand the sight of demons anymore."

"Sure thing."

"I'll let everyone know that we're in position." Jophiel held out her hand and spoke into the orb. "Omegas, this is Jophiel the Auburn. Allōs and I are in position. Report."

"Jophiel, this is Gabriel the Gold. We are in position and ready to go. Report back when everything starts catching fire."

"Will do."

I calmed my mind and closed my eyes. I could see everything around me – the cross, the streets, the buildings, and Jophiel to my right. I searched for the remaining crosses by locking onto their heat signatures. I sensed them all, and I started breathing. I felt the temperature rise and fall with my breath. I kept breathing, taking deeper and deeper breaths. I raised my arms with every inhale and lowered them on the exhale. The flames didn't burn with sadness or hatred; they burned peacefully. I opened my eyes.

"Let's do this, in the name of God the Father, the Son and the Holy Spirit, Amen!" I made the sign of the cross in the air and swiped my arm up. The cross in front of me exploded into a large blue column. All the demons surrounding us were instantly vaporized. I poured all of the energy I could into letting the flames rage. The column in front of me grew larger and larger. The heat from the flames set everything around it on fire and soon everywhere I looked was consumed by flames. The wails of demons permeated the air and made my skin crawl. The cry of demons started to fizzle out and then only the rumble of the flames could be heard.

"Jophiel, so what happens to Earth after this?"

"I couldn't tell you even if I wanted to. God might place everyone back when we're finished, but I genuinely don't know."

A small orb appeared in front of us. I tapped it and a ghostly image of Gabriel appeared before me.

"Allōs, it's completely quiet here. Snuff out the flames and meet me at Dunmore beach."

"With pleasure, Gabe." I inhaled and with a divisive downward motion, the flames disappeared. It smelled like death and burning wood. I said, "I hope I can return to Earth. It was quite lovely living here."

"I will admit it was fun seeing what humans could come up with," Jophiel said. "Now let's meet up with the others."

We teleported back to Dunmore beach.

The others were waiting for us.

"Great job, Al! You really did me proud."

"Thanks, Gabe." I looked over and saw Luke lying in the sand.

"Al, I'm so sorry," Noah said. He placed his hand on my shoulder.

I pulled him into my arms and cried, "I know you are, Noah."

"Just breathe, Al."

"I don't know if I'll ever see them again."

"I know you'll see Jamie again, Al. I have a good feeling about that. And as for Luke, you'll find a way to see him again."

"You think so?"

"I know so. Now, Al, clean yourself up. You're a bloody mess and we have to go to a funeral soon, so try not to make a fool of yourself."

"So I can't throw myself in Luke's casket?"

"Do you really want to be that guy?"

"I'd rather not. Come on, let's head home."

"He's right. We need to prepare for Luke's funeral," Gabriel said.

"Let me bring Jamie, please?"

Gabriel smiled and nodded. "Take us to him."

I led the Omegas to the pub and they were taken aback by the amount of blood that was splattered about. At the base of the bar, Jamie lay dead underneath a blanket in a pool of blood.

"Lord have mercy on his soul," Ariel said, as she covered her mouth in shock.

"Dear God," commented Azrael.

Chamuel shielded his eyes. "Allōs, I'm so sorry," he said. "It's a beautiful pub though. Jamie really loved this place, didn't he?"

"He really did, Chamuel, and so did the town. We were busy every night for months."

"What happened to Jamie?" Jophiel asked.

"I don't know the specifics, but all I know is that Jamie was killed by Lucifer."

"He also took a blow to the chest. It was a bladed weapon. He died of blood loss," Michael chimed in, as he inspected Jamie.

"So Lucifer cut him open?" Gabriel asked.

"Looks like it, based off of the cut across his shirt. The interesting part is someone tried to heal him, but they were too late. Al, is this your handiwork?"

"Yes. Jamie didn't want me to heal him completely. He just wanted me to be with him."

"Did something happen to his neck?"

"That's enough. Leave him be, Michael, please. I don't have the heart to see anymore," I said, as my voice cracked.

"I'm sorry, Allōs, that was inappropriate of me. I am truly sorry for your losses."

"You talk as if this is only going to affect me."

Gabriel said, "It's going to hit us all hard, Allōs. Now let's go home."

"Okay, Gabe. Luke! Shit! He's still at the beach!"

Ariel snapped her fingers and Luke appeared in her arms. I gazed at Luke's lifeless face.

"I will miss you so much, my love. Wherever you are, please let me know that you're still with me. Ariel, hand me Luke."

"Al, that would be too cruel of me to let you do that."

"You're probably right." I picked up Jamie and we all vanished and returned to Gabriel's chambers.

The smell of cigar smoke filled the room. It put me at ease. *I'm home. It's good to be back.* I felt the sadness start to creep in, but I fought the urge to cry. My eyes began to swell; I blinked and felt a tear roll down my cheek.

"Where would you like me to put Jamie?"

Jophiel waved her hand and a stone table appeared. I gently rested Jamie on the table and pulled the blanket from his face. I looked at Jamie's face and he looked like he was at peace. I couldn't help but smile.

"Jamie, I'm glad I could comfort you in your final moments."

"I will call Peter," Gabriel said morosely.

I tapped my chest and my armor receded into my skin. I took Luke from Ariel's arms and sat down in a chair with him draped over my lap. I tapped his chest and his armor receded into his diamond ring.

"When an angel dies, his or her ring will disconnect from the body and then and only then will it be able to be taken off," I whispered, as I slid off Luke's ring. "Does anyone have a problem with me taking this?"

"It's yours."

"Thank you, Michael."

Peter came knocking at the door with two blank stone

caskets. I placed Luke in his casket, and then removed the blanket over Jamie and placed him into his. I said, "May I have a moment with these two?"

The Omegas nodded, and they went into the hallway.

"Knock on the door when you're ready, Allōs," Gabriel said, as he closed the door behind him.

"Luke, may I cry now?" Tears trickled down my face. "I can't believe you're really gone. You scared the hell out of me when we first started fighting together. I remember when you, Noah, and I were just entry-level angels and we barely made it out alive on our first mission. I thought you were going to die then, but you pushed through. I know I'm asking this in vain, but please open those green eyes of yours, babe. There won't be a day that I won't think of you. We have been to Hell and back. I will gladly venture there once more to bring you back. I will find a way, I promise."

I fidgeted with Luke's ring. I put it in my pocket and I turned to Jamie. "Jamie, I think you had the worst end of the deal. You were tortured and then gutted like a fish and what did you get in return? Death and despair. I know you weren't religious, but I believe that you'll end up here in Heaven. You know why I think that? You've shown me kindness that I never thought humans could show. More importantly, you accepted me when I gave you the truth. I just hope you believed it." I wiped away my tears and looked at both of them and said, "Now go, both of you. Fly into the arms of God. Luke, my love, I will make sure that I see you again. As for you, Jamie, I will see you soon. I have a good feeling about that. When you get to Heaven, please allow God to heal you, I beg of you. Jamie, you've experienced far more pain than anyone should in a lifetime. I'll be looking for you, Jamie, and to help with that I have one more tattoo to add to your collection."

I placed my hand on the left side of his chest and it started to glow, revealing an omega sign encased in a circle on top of his shirt. The crest sunk beneath the fabric and shone through his shirt. I felt my brand start to sting. When Jamie's crest went dull, the pain in my chest subsided. "Both of you, rest easy, until we meet again."

I knocked on the door and the Omegas came in and we went to the funeral.

Months passed, and I still couldn't get over the trauma of what had happened. I thought visiting Luke's and Jamie's graves would help me cope, but ultimately it did not. Each time I came to their graves, I always admired the artistry of the stone carvings that covered their caskets. The sculptures were so lifelike. The artists had captured every detail from the way that Luke had styled his hair to Jamie's eyebrow piercing. I gently ran my fingers over Luke's effigy.

"I will find a way to bring you back." I felt someone's presence behind me. I turned around and it was Mother.

"You fought well, Allōs. You should be very proud of yourself."

"I don't feel proud, Mother."

"Why's that?"

"Well, I lost the love of my life and a very good friend. Not to mention that I failed to contain Ovelth. Mother, where am I supposed to go from here?" Mother hugged me.

"You'll be staying here and I'll be keeping an extra careful eye on you. But, Allōs, you should be proud. I love you."

"I love you too." Mother left, leaving me with my thoughts. Ovelth appeared in front of me.

"Do you really think that you can contain me?"

"Contain you, no."

Ovelth cracked a wicked smile as he swirled around me.

"Good, you cannot stop—"

I interrupted Ovelth.

"But I will kill you."

CPSIA information can be obtained
at www.ICGtesting.com
Printed in the USA
LVHW040113060822
725039LV00003B/11

9 781800 420816